ZOMBIES

Geronimo nearly gagged as a putrid stench filled the air. He backpedaled as more Zombies poured from the abandoned vehicles.

Something collided with his back.

Geronimo whirled, and found Blade alongside him. "What do we do?" he asked.

The Technics opened up with their Dakon IIs, their fragmentation bullets tearing into the hissing Zombies and ripping them apart, blowing their chests and skulls to shreds or tearing limbs from bodies. Greenish fluid sprayed everywhere.

The Zombies never broke stride. Their grisly arms extended, their yellow fingernails glinting in the sunlight, their thin lips quivering in anticipation of their next meal. . . .

DAVID ROBBINS

ENDWORLD

NEW YORK RUN

LEISURE BOOKS ∞ NEW YORK CITY

Dedicated to
Judy and Joshua
in eternal love . . .
to the memory of Ian Fleming;
no one will ever do it better . . .
or as well . . .
and to Napoleon Solo and Illya Kuryakin,
who were right all along.

A LEISURE BOOK

published by

Dorchester Publishing Co., Inc.
6 East 39th Street
New York, NY 10016

Printed in the United States of America

FOREWORD

It is 100 years after World War III. Give or take a year.

The good news? The planet is still here.

The bad news? The planet is still here.

The massive radiation and the staggering array of chemical-warfare weaponry unleashed on the globe precipitated an environmental disaster of incalculable proportions. In the U.S., much of the soil has been contaminated beyond reclamation, principally in the vicinity of nuclear strike zones, "hot spots." The climate has been altered; former fertile land might be withered dust, while former dry areas might receive an abundance of rainfall. The wildlife and human gene pool has been drastically affected by the radiation and the chemicals. Mutations are commonplace. Giantism increasingly frequent. The landscape is overrun by savage creatures of every conceivable shape and size.

Civilization is on the verge of complete collapse.

Chaos rules.

Almost.

Lingering outposts of humanity are resisting the rising tide of darkness, stubbornly clinging to the old ways or forging new paths of progressive development.

In the forefront of the strengthening forces of light, at the vanguard of the effort to reassert mankind as the dominant species on the planet, is the Freedom Federation. Comprised of a loose confederation of disparate groups, the Freedom Federation is valiantly striving to reestablish order in a world gone mad. Six factions constitute the Federation:

The Civilized Zone is the official title for a section in the Midwest embracing the former states of Kansas. Nebraska, Colorado, Wyoming, New Mexico, Oklahoma, portions of Arizona and the northern half of Texas. The government evacuated thousands of its citizens into this region during the war. Denver, Colorado, spared a direct hit during the conflict, became the new capital.

Montana has become the exclusive domain of the Flathead Indians, free at last from the white man's yoke.

The Dakota territory is the home of superb horsemen known as the Cavalry.

In northern Minnesota, deep underground, secure in their subterranean city, reside the people known as the Moles.

Also in northern Minnesota, in the former town of Halma, live the refugees from the Twin Cities called the Clan.

And finally, not far from Halma, on the outskirts of Lake Bronson State Park, in a survivalist compound constructed by a wealthy filmmaker named Kurt Carpenter immediately prior to the war, dwells the smallest faction in the Freedom Federation—but the one with the most influence. Carpenter's descendants are called the Family, and their 30-acre compound is known as the home. Like the Spartans of antiquity, they are renowned for two features: their wise leadership and their fearless fighters. The 15 Family members responsible for the defense of the Home and the preservation of the Family, collectively called the Warriors, have established a reputation for valor in combat matched by few others.

Several of the Warriors have ventured into uncharted realms east of the Civilized Zone. They've discovered that the city of St. Louis has become the turf of an outlaw motorcycle gang, the Leather Knights. And they've learned that the Russians have control of a corridor running through the center of the eastern half of the country.

They've also heard about other . . . things.

Evil things. Menacing things. Things better left alone. Things to be avoided at all costs.

Unless they come calling at your door . . .

1

The four members of Elite Squad-A7 could sense their impending doom in the dank air.

"Readings!" Captain Edwards barked, struggling to keep his voice under control.

The trooper with the pulse scanner strapped to his right wrist, Private Dougherty, was gaping down the dim passage to their right.

"Scan, damnit!" Captain Edwards ordered, slapping Dougherty on the left shoulder.

The youthful Dougherty, sweat beading his brow and coating his crewcut brown hair under his helmet, took a deep breath and glanced down at his scanner. "They're still after us!" he wailed. "Coming from every direction!"

"How many?" Captain Edwards demanded.

Dougherty shook his head. "I can't tell! There's too much interference!"

"We can't stay here!" Captain Edwards declared. "We're too exposed."

Elite Squad-A7 was silhouetted in the junction of two hallways, their shadows projected along the tiled walls by their helmet lamps.

"Stick together!" Captain Edwards commanded. "We can't afford to be separated!"

Private Dougherty and the two others, Geisz and Winkel, nodded their understanding, their helmet lamps bobbing up and down.

Captain Edwards took the passage to his left. His

palms felt sweaty on the Dakon II fragmentation rifle clutched in his hands.

"I've got a blip twenty yards behind us!" Private Dougherty yelled.

The four commandos spun, facing toward the junction they'd just vacated.

"On me!" Captain Edwards bellowed, leveling the Dakon II, his finger on the trigger.

Their combined lamp lights clearly illuminated the junction. A shadowy apparition appeared for an instant, and they caught a glimpse of a tall creature with grimy, gray flesh, gaping, reddish eyes, and a leering mouthful of yellow teeth. The monstrosity stopped and blinked in the bright light, starting to step backward, raising its left arm to shield its moldy face.

"Fire!" Captain Edwards shouted.

The passageway thundered as the four members of Elite Squad-A7 opened up, their fragmentation rifles chattering in unison.

The creature in the junction was struck in the chest and head, its body exploding in a violent spray of putrid flesh and a vile, greenish fluid. It shrieked as it died.

"Move!" Captain Edwards instructed his squad.

Geisz and Winkel took off, Geisz taking the point, her blue eyes alertly scanning the corridor ahead.

Private Dougherty followed them, studying the scanner.

Captain Edwards brought up the rear. "Readings!" he snapped.

"They've disappeared off the scope," Dougherty replied.

"That's impossible!" Captain Edwards responded.

"I'm telling you they're gone!" Private Dougherty said, disputing his superior.

"Let me see that!" Captain Edwards said.

Private Dougherty halted and swung his right arm around. "Here! See for yourself."

Captain Edwards leaned over the scanner, checking the grids for blips of white light.

Nothing.

"But that's impossible," Edwards repeated.

"Don't I know it!" Dougherty agreed.

"Let's go!" Captain Edwards kept his lamplight on the hallway behind them as he trailed Dougherty, his mind whirling. There was no way they could just vanish like that! So where the hell had they gone? Were there other passages or vents not marked on the blueprints the Technics possessed? Some way they could travel beyond scanner range in the space of a few seconds?

"Captain Edwards!" came a cry from further along the hall.

Edwards recognized the voice of Marion Geisz. "Hurry!" he prodded Dougherty, and the two of them hastened along the corridor.

Geisz and Winkel were waiting ahead, their helmet lamps pointed downward.

They'd found the stairwell. Again.

"It looks like there's no bottom," Geisz commented as Edwards and Dougherty reached her side.

"It gives me the creeps!" Winkel commented, his brown eyes wide from fright.

"Stow that crap, mister!" Captain Edwards stated. He stared down the stairwell, noting the dusty metal rails and the cobwebs covering the walls. "We know our objective, people! Let's get cracking! Geisz, the point!"

"What else?" Geisz quipped, and started down.

"I just hope the Minister was right about this place," Winkel said as he followed Geisz.

"Can the squawking!" Captain Edwards ordered. "You know better! You're the best of the best!" he reminded them. "Technic commandos! Act like it!"

The three troopers took the reprimand in resentful silence. Geisz, in particular, was irritated by Edwards' audacity. She'd seen far more combat than he had, and she knew what was expected of a professional storm trooper. Still, now was hardly the time to be distracted by petty animosities. She had to concentrate on the task at hand, or she might not live to see Chicago again. Moisture was trickling from under her helmet, plastering her crewcut blonde hair to her scalp, causing her skin to itch. She suppressed an impulse to scratch the itching, and focused on the stairs ahead.

Dust and spiderwebs.

And more dust and spiderwebs.

But nothing else.

Geisz saw the streaks of dust caking the metal railings, and suddenly realized there wasn't any dust on the stairs.

Someone . . . or something . . . must be using the stairs on a regular basis, but not bothering to use the railings.

Three guesses what they were.

Geisz reached up and cranked the volume control on her right ear amplifier. There was a crackling in her helmet, then a sustained hiss as the transistorized microphone strained for all its circuits were worth.

What was that?

Private Geisz slowed, listening intently. She thought she'd heard the muffled tread of a foot on the stairs below. She leaned over the railing and swept the lower levels with her lamp.

Nothing.

"Anything?" Captain Edwards asked from up above.

"I don't know," Geisz replied uncertainly.

"Stay alert!" Captain Edwards advised them.

Geisz almost laughed. As if they had to be told! She cautiously took another turn in the stairwell, walking to the right, her Dakon II at the ready.

Something scraped below her.

Geisz stopped, leaning against the wall to protect her back.

"What is it?" Captain Edwards demanded.

Geisz ignored him, striving to pinpoint the source of the noise.

"What is it?" Captain Edwards asked again. "Why the holdup?"

Geisz motioned for quiet. She could detect the faint sound of heavy breathing in her right ear.

"I'm getting something!" Dougherty suddenly yelled. "Lots of them! Above and below us! And . . ." he paused.

"And?" Captain Edwards angrily goaded him.

"And on both sides!" Dougherty said.

"Both sides?" Captain Edwards surveyed the stairwell. "There's nothing there but brick walls!"

"This damn thing must be broken," Dougherty muttered, adjusting the calibration control on his pulse scanner.

It wasn't.

The wall behind Private Dougherty abruptly collapsed, tumbling bricks and mortar onto the stairs and creating a swirling cloud of dust.

"What the . . .!" Captain Edwards began, and then he spotted the forms pouring from the gaping hole in the stairwell wall.

Dougherty saw them too, and he cut loose with his fragmentation rifle, the dumdum bullets ripping into the nightmarish creatures and blowing their grisly bodies apart. He downed two, three, four in swift succession, and then one of them reached him. Momentarily paralyzed with fear, he screamed as a cold, clammy, moist hand closed on his throat.

Captain Edwards saw the hulking figure towering over Dougherty, but he hesitated, unwilling to risk hitting the trooper. The cloud of dust reduced visibility to only a few feet, and he wanted to be sure before he pulled the trigger. He moved in closer, aiming his rifle, when strong hands clamped on his shoulders and lifted him bodily from the floor.

Private Geisz, enveloped in the dust, tried to catch a glimpse of her companions. She saw several struggling forms in the middle of the dust cloud, then felt her blood freeze as a terrifying screech reverberated in the confines of the gloomy stairwell.

There was a loud, crunching noise, like the sound of breaking bones.

"Captain Edwards!" Geisz shouted. "Doughboy! Wink! What's happening?"

No one answered.

A tall scarecrow shape loomed above her, its stick-like limbs clawing in her direction.

Something growled.

Private Geisz cowered against the wall, her

meticulous training overwhelmed by her instinctive loathing of the form on the step above. She could see one bony hand reaching for her neck, could see its wrinkled, gray flesh and its tapered, yellow nails, and could even see the brown dirt caked between its extended fingers. She wanted to bolt, to flee for her life, to get the hell out of there. But at the very second when those gruesome fingers touched her skin, instead of racing pell-mell down the stairs in reckless flight and abandoning her mates and friends, she reached deep within herself and discovered her innermost self, her true nature, her fundamental essence, the steel of her personality. Her bravery was tested to its limits, and she wasn't found lacking.

"Eat this, sucker!" Geisz stated defiantly, and angled the Dakon II toward the creature's midsection.

The creature hissed.

Geisz squeezed the trigger.

Her attacker was blown backward by the impact of the dumdum bullets, its body bursting apart across the chest and face.

Geisz didn't bother to check it; she knew the damn thing was dead. She punched the Dakon II onto full automatic and bounded up the stairs, into the dispersing dust cloud, searching for her companions.

Figures were all around her in the gloom.

"Captain!" Geisz yelled. As the last of the cloud dissipated, her helmet lamp revealed the hideous features of those nearest her. With a start, she realized she was completely surrounded by . . . them! There was no sign of her fellow commandos!

One of the creatures lunged at her, its red orbs glaring.

Geisz crouched against the railing and fired, swinging the Dakon II in an arc from right to left, taking out everything in her field of vision. She saw more monstrosities coming from the hole in the wall and fired into them, the fragmentation rifle functioning flawlessly, ripping them apart, literally blasting their shriveled flesh from their bones.

They fell in droves.

One of them was advancing down the stairs toward her.

Geisz spun to shoot them, but the Dakon II unexpectedly went empty.

Oh, no!

Geisz frantically released the spent magazine and heard it clatter on the stairs as she extracted a fresh magazine from her belt pouch and hurriedly inserted it into the rifle. She slapped her left hand on the bottom of the new clip, slamming it home, and she shot the creature in the face even as it sprang at her.

Suddenly, she was alone.

Geisz realized the creatures were gone. She scanned the hole, then up and down the stairwell. Bodies littered the steps, but none of them belonged to her friends or the captain.

What the hell had happened to them?

Geisz pondered her next move. If she were smart, she'd head for the surface and the jeep and take off for Chicago. But what if Doughboy and Wink and Edwards were still alive? Didn't she owe it to them to try and find them? She thoughtfully bit her lower lip. Yeah, she owed it to them. But how was she supposed to find them? The tunnels under the city were a virtual maze. Doughboy had carried their scanner, and without the pulse scanner she couldn't get a fix on their belt frequencies. She frowned, disgusted. Why the hell hadn't they issued scanners to everyone? She knew the answer to that one. The higher-ups wanted their arms free so they could carry more of the stuff up to the jeep.

And what about the stuff? The objective of their mission?

Geisz stared down the stairwell. It was down there, according to the Minister. About two floors below her present position. Canister after canister of it. Was the stuff worth so many lives? she wondered.

She had a choice to make.

Geisz shook her head in frustration. Either she could search for Edwards, Doughboy, and Wink, when she knew there wasn't a chance of locating them, or she could retrieve one of the damned canisters for the Minister.

Crap.

Private Geisz stood and moved down the stairwell, treading softly, her right ear tuned to the amplifier in her helmet. She descended two floors to the lowest level without incident.

So where were the creatures?

She leaned against the wall at the bottom of the stairwell and played her light over the passageway ahead. What was it Doughboy had called the things? Zombies! That was it.

So where were the Zombies?

Geisz detected a doorway about 30 feet away, in the right-hand wall. On an impulse, she replaced the partially spent magazine with a new one from her pouch. There was no sense in being careless at this point of the game! She insured the Dakon was set on full automatic, then pressed the proper button to activate the Laser Sighting Mode. Sure, it would be a drain on the batteries, but she couldn't afford to waste precious time sighting the rifle, especially now that she was alone. The red dots could be a lifesaver when every millisecond counted.

Here goes nothing!

Private Geisz sidled toward the doorway, keeping her back against the right wall. Her head was constantly in motion, sweeping her helmet light along the corridor. Static crackled in her right ear. She glanced at the tiled floor, then stopped, perplexed.

Dust covered the floor and the walls, a thick layer of dust undisturbed by a solitary footprint.

Something was wrong here.

Geisz examined the floor for as far as her light revealed, and it was all the same. Not a single print. But why? she asked herself. The Zombies were all over the place. They infested the ruins. Why didn't they use this hallway? Why did they apparently avoid the lower level? There was no evidence of anyone, or anything, using this corridor in a long, long time.

Why?

Geisz grinned. What was the matter with her? Why was she looking a gift horse in the mouth? If the Zombies weren't down here, so much the better! It made her job that much easier! She walked to the doorway and paused before the closed wooden door.

What if they were waiting for her on the other side?

Geisz pressed the right side of her helmet against the door and listened, but the amplifier was silent.

Lady Luck was with her!

Geisz tried the knob, and wasn't surprised to find it locked. She took a step back, then spun, ramming her right leg into the door, her black boot slamming into the wood an inch from the knob. The door trembled, but it held. She kicked at it again, and again, and on her third attempt the aged wood splintered and cracked and the door swung open.

There was a rustling sound from inside the inky interior.

Geisz flattened against the wall and tensed.

Now what?

Geisz felt goosebumps erupt all over her flesh, and she resisted an urge to run. She wasn't about to quit when she was this close to their objective! Besides, all she needed was one lousy canister and the Minister would hail her as a hero. It might even mean a promotion, and she could use the extra pay.

She took a deep breath.

Geisz crouched and whirled into the doorway, the Dakon II pointed into the chamber, her helmet lamp illuminating the room and its contents.

The canister chamber was perhaps 20 feet square, and crammed with stack after stack of faded yellow canisters. The canisters, six inches in diameter and ten inches in height, were stacked in tidy rows from the cement floor to the ceiling.

All except in the center.

Geisz took a step forward. The middle of the chamber was covered with piles of fallen canisters, as if dozens of stacks had collapsed. All things considered, it was a minor miracle all of the stacks hadn't toppled over when the city was hit.

So what had made the rustling sound?

Geisz looked around the chamber, but nothing moved. She decided to grab a canister and scoot. Taking more than one was impossible. She would have her hands full fighting the Zombies en route to the surface. One would be burden enough. She hastened to the nearest stack, reached up, and took hold of one of the canisters. As she did, her helmet lamp focused on the ceiling, on the center of the ceiling directly above the collapsed stacks in the middle of the room.

It was perched in a huge hole in the ceiling, its legs bent, prepared to pounce.

Geisz gasped at the sight of it, stunned.

One of its four green eyes blinked.

Geisz backpedaled, elevating the Dakon II, a sinking sensation in the pit of her stomach.

The size of it!

She reached the doorway, and that's when the thing dropped toward her, roaring, its ten legs scrambling over the canisters and upending stack after stack as it surged after her.

Geisz crouched and squeezed the trigger, the Dakon II cradled in her right arm. The fragmentation bullets tore into the deviate, rocking it, chunks and bits of black flesh and shredded skin flying in every direction. The chamber shook as it reared up and bellowed in agony.

But it kept coming.

Geisz turned and ran, heading for the stairwell. She glanced over her left shoulder, knowing the thing couldn't possibly squeeze its gigantic bulk through the narrow doorway, confident she could escape before it breached the door. So she was all the more amazed when it flowed through the doorway without breaking its stride, its body seeming to contract as it passed through and expanding again once it was in the corridor.

No!

Geisz raced for her life, her heart pounding in her chest. She reached the stairwell and gripped the railing, risking one quick look down the hallway.

It was only a foot away, its cavernous maw wide, its fangs glistening in the light from her lamp.

Geisz swung the Dakon II up, the red dot clearly visible on the mutant's sloping forehead, and pulled the trigger.

The deviate roared and closed in.

Private Marion Geisz fired as the thing reached for her, fired as its claws clamped on her abdomen, and fired as it lifted her into the air and her stomach was crushed to a pulp. Her arms went limp, and blood poured from her mouth. She sagged and dropped the Dakon II, and the last sight she saw was the monster's teeth snapping at her face.

She thought she heard someone screaming.

2

The child was 18 months old, a stocky boy with full cheeks, impish blue eyes, and curly blond hair. He stared up at his father with an intensity belying his tender age.

"Now this is called a Colt Python," said the man, twirling the pearl-handled revolver in his right hand. "One day, these guns could be yours." He twirled the Colt in his left hand, then slid both Pythons into their respective holsters with a practiced flourish. To even a casual observer, the boy's lineage would have been obvious. The father was a tall, lean blond with long hair and a flowing moustache. His blue eyes seemed to twinkle with an inner light, reflecting a keen zest for life. The gunman wore buckskins and moccasins, as did the child. "Are you payin' attention to all of this, Ringo?" he asked the boy.

Ringo dutifully nodded, then grinned. "Ringo potty."

The gunman's mouth dropped. "What?"

"Ringo potty pease," the boy said.

"Blast!" The gunman grabbed his son and darted toward a nearby cabin. "Your mother's gonna kill me if I don't get you there on time." He jogged to the cabin, opened a door in the west wall, and dashed inside.

As the door was closing, another man appeared on the scene. He was huge, his powerful physique bulging with layers of muscles, his arms rippling as he moved. A black leather vest, green fatigue pants, and black boots scarcely covered his awesome frame. Twin Bowie knives were strapped around his stout waist. His dark hair hung down over his gray eyes. Smiling, he strolled up to the cabin door and knocked.

"Who the blazes is it?" came a muffled response.

"Blade," the giant announced.

"I'm busy!"

"I'll bet you are," Blade said, chuckling. "I can wait."

"This might take a while, pard," yelled the gunman.

"I can wait," Blade reiterated. He leaned upon the rough wall and idly crossed his massive arms at chest height. This was the life! he told himself. Taking it easy. Enjoying his wife and son and discharging his responsibilities as head Warrior with a minimum of fuss. The fewer hassles, the better. A robin alighted in a maple tree at the west end of the cabin. A squirrel crisscrossed the ground 15 yards away. The scene was tranquil and soothing.

As life should be.

The cabin door was jerked open, the gunman framed in the doorway with a diaper clutched in his right hand. "Is this important?" he demanded. "I'm kind of tied up at the moment."

Blade grinned. "So I see. Did you reach the toilet in time?"

"You saw, huh?" the gunman asked sheepishly.

"I think I'm going to nominate you for daddy of the year," Blade joked.

Little Ringo waddled into view between the gunman's legs, his pants down around his ankles, his privates exposed to the world.

"Hi, Ringo," Blade cheerfully greeted him. "Is Hickok behaving himself?"

Ringo looked up at his father. "Ringo pee-pee," he said in his high voice.

"Now?" Hickok inquired.

Ringo nodded and proceeded to urinate all over the floor and Hickok's moccasins.

"Blast!" Hickok said, taking hold of his son and scrambling toward the bathroom.

Blade laughed. "You sure you know what you're doing?" he called out.

"Funny! Funny! Funny!" was the muttered reply from the bathroom.

"I don't know if Sherry should leave you alone with Ringo," Blade taunted his friend. "It could be hazardous to the boy's health."

"What about you, pard?" Hickok rejoined. "How come Jenny let you out of the house without your leash?"

"She's over at Geronimo's," Blade answered. "Where's your wife?"

"She went to see the Tillers about an extra allotment of veggies for Ringo," Hickok revealed. "He had the runs, and the Healers said he needs more greens in his diet."

"Gabriel had the runs last week," Blade said. "He's better now," he added, referring to his own son.

Hickok emerged from the bathroom a minute later with Ringo in tow. There was a distinct bulge on the left side of the boy's pants.

"Are you certain you put that diaper on correctly?" Blade asked.

Hickok glanced at his son. "Yeah. Why?"

"It doesn't look right," Blade said.

"You're just jealous 'cause you can't do it as good as me," Hickok retorted.

A slim, blonde woman, wearing a brown leather shirt and faded, patched jeans, walked around the east end of the cabin. A Smith and Wesson .357 Combat Magnum was belted around her narrow waist. "Hi, Blade," she greeted the towering Warrior.

"Hi, Sherry," Blade said to Hickok's wife.

Sherry's green eyes narrowed as they fell on Ringo. She shot an annoyed glare in the guman's direction. "What's wrong with his diaper?"

"He just went potty," Hickok stated proudly. "And I got him there in time. Well, almost in time."

"What did you do to his diaper?" Sherry reiterated.

"Nothin'. Why?"

Sherry knelt and tapped the bulge in Ringo's pants.

"What'd you put in there? A rock?"

"I just put on a new diaper," Hickok stated.

"What kind of knot did you use?" Sherry inquired.

"What does it matter?" Hickok said defensively.

"What kind of knot?" Sherry asked insistently.

"A timber hitch," Hickok mumbled.

"A what?"

"A timber hitch," Hickok declared. "I'm good at timber hitches."

Sherry glanced at Blade, rolled her eyes, and sighed. She picked up Ringo and stalked into the cabin. "How many times do I have to tell you," she said over her right shoulder, "you don't use timber hitches on a cloth diaper."

"So what's the big deal over a teensy-weensy knot?" Hickok wanted to know. "The diaper stays on, doesn't it?"

"Men!" Sherry exclaimed as she walked into the bathroom.

"Women!" Hickok muttered as he stepped outside and closed the cabin door. He looked at Blade. "So what's up?"

"Plato wants to see us," Blade said.

"How come?" Hickok asked as they strolled to the west.

"The Freedom Federation is going to have another conference," Blade disclosed. "The leaders are going to meet here in a couple of months, and Plato wants to go over our security arrangements."

Hickok snickered. "Just like the old-timer to get all frazzled about somethin' two months away!"

"Don't refer to Plato as an old-timer," Blade said testily.

"Why not?"

"You should treat Plato with more respect," Blade stated.

"I respect Plato," Hickok said sincerely. "But when a man is pushin' fifty, and he's got long, gray hair down to his shoulders, and more wrinkles on his face than there are cracks in the mud of a dry creek bed, then I reckon he qualifies for old-timer status."

"Plato is the Family Leader," Blade said archly. "He deserves our courtesy and consideration."

"But that doesn't mean I've gotta kiss his tootsies," the gunman remarked.

Blade sighed. "You're incorrigible, you know that?"

"Yep." Hickok nodded. "My missus tells me that at least once a day."

"She's right," Blade said.

The two Warriors were approaching the concrete block nearest the row of cabins, and Blade gazed at the compound ahead, marveling once again at how well the Founder had built the Home.

Kurt Carpenter had spent millions on the survivalist retreat. Square in shape, enclosed by brick walls 20 feet in height and topped with barbed wire, the Home was a model of efficiency and organization. The eastern half of the compound was preserved in its natural state and devoted to agricultural pursuits. In the middle of the Home, aligned from north to south in a straight line, were the cabins reserved for married Family members. The western section was the socializing area and the site of the large concrete bunkers—or blocks, as the Family called them. Arranged in a triangular formation, there were six in all. The first, A Block, was the Family armory and the southern tip of the triangle. B Block came 100 yards to the northwest of A Block, and it was the sleeping quarters for single Family members and the gathering place for community functions. C Block was 100 yards northwest of B Block, and it served as the infirmary for the Family Healers, members rigorously trained in herbal and holistic medicine. D Block, 100 yards east of C Block, was the Family workshop for everything from carpentry to metalworking. Next in line, 100 yards east of D Block, was E Block, the enormous Family library personally stocked with hundreds of thousands of books by Kurt Carpenter. Carpenter had foreseen the value knowledge would acquire in a world stripped of its educational institutions. Consequently, Carpenter had stocked books on every conceivable subject in the library. These precious volumes, frayed and faded after a century of use, were the Family's most cherished possessions. Finally, 100 yards southwest of the library was F Block, utilized for gardening, farming, and food-processing purposes.

The entire compound was surrounded by the brick walls and one additional line of defense: an interior moat, a rechanneled stream, entering the retreat under the northwestern corner and diverted in both directions along the base of the four walls, finally exiting the compound underneath the southeastern corner. Access to the Home was over a drawbridge positioned in the center of the west wall, a drawbridge designed to lower outward. Traversal of the moat was accomplished via a massive bridge between the drawbridge and the compound proper.

The cleared space between the six blocks was filled with Family members: families on picnics, children playing, lovers arm in arm, others chatting or singing or engaged in athletic activities.

"Who's on wall duty?" Hickok inquired.

"Beta Triad," Blade replied. The 15 Family Warriors were divided into 5 fighting units, or Triads, of 3 Warriors apiece. Designated as Alpha, Beta, Gamma, Omega, and Zulu, they rotated guard assignments and their other responsibilities during times of peace, but functioned collectively during any conflict and fought as a precision force during times of war.

Hickok, scanning the rampart on the west wall, nodded. "I can seek Rikki," he mentioned. Rikki-Tikki-Tavi was the head of Beta Triad. His Beta mates, Yama and Teucer, would be patrolling the other walls.

"I see Plato," Blade commented.

The wizened Family Leader was standing near the wooden bridge, his hands clasped behind his wiry frame, his gray hair whipping in the breeze of the August day.

"So what's the big deal about security arrangements for a conference two months from now?" Hickok absently asked.

"We'll find out in a minute," Blade said, and the pair made their way toward Plato.

A stocky Indian, dressed in green pants and a green shirt, with a genuine tomahawk tucked under his deer-hide belt and slanted across his right thigh, jogged in their direction.

Hickok beamed. "Looks like Geronimo's wife decided to let him get some fresh air."

Geronimo reached them and nodded. "I've been looking for you two."

"Why? Did you miss me?" Hickok asked playfully.

Geronimo, his brown eyes twinkling, feigned shock. "Miss you? Why would anyone in their right mind miss a monumental pain in the butt like you?" He ran his left hand through his short, black hair and, disguised by the motion of his left arm, winked at Blade.

Hickok touched his chest. "You've hurt me to the quick," he said in mock pain.

"To the quick?" Geronimo reiterated playfully. "If I didn't know better, I'd swear you've been reading some Shakespeare."

Hickok's nose crinkled distastefully. "Shakespeare? Are you joshing me or what? Give me Louis L'Amour any day of the week."

"*Aha*!" Geronimo exclaimed. "So you admit you can read!"

"I can read as good as you!" Hickok retorted. "I attended the same Family school you did, dummy!" He paused. "Why?"

"Because," Geronimo said, his full features radiating his impending triumph in their continual war of words, "anyone who talks like you do and acts like you do had to pick up their stupidity somewhere! And I know you don't come by it naturally, because I knew your parents and they were both normal."

Blade laughed. As his fellow Alpha Triad members and lifelong friends, Hickok and Geronimo were constantly at each other's throats. The lean gunman and his shorter partner were known to enjoy an abiding affection, the kind of friendship you only find once or twice in a lifetime. They were spiritual brothers, usually inseparable, and decidedly deadly when working in concert. Blade was grateful they were in his Triad.

The trio neared Plato.

"How's Ringo doing?" Geronimo asked Hickok.

"Fine," Hickok said, grinning. "He's a chip off the old block."

"Poor kid," Geronimo mumbled.

Plato turned as they reached him. His aged frame was clothed in an old, yellow shirt with a leather patch on both elbows and worn, brown pants. "Hello," he greeted them. "Thank you for coming."

"Blade's wife said you wanted to see all of us," Geronimo said.

Plato nodded. "We must discuss the Freedom Federation conference."

"But it's not for two months yet," Hickok stated.

"I don't believe in leaving important details until the very last minute," Plato said earnestly.

"We had a conference here about six months ago," Blade said. "We didn't have any problems then. All we had to do was post additional Warriors on the walls."

"True," Plato admitted. "But I've received a most disturbing communication from Wolfe."

Blade's piercing, gray eyes narrowed. Wolfe was the leader of the Moles, dwellers in a subterranean city located over 50 miles southeast of the Home. "When did you get word from Wolfe?"

"Late last night," Plato said. "His messenger arrived after you had retired, and I didn't see the need to awaken you."

"Where's this messenger now?" Geronimo asked.

"Sleeping in B Block," Plato said. "He was extremely fatigued from the journey. After he delivered his report, we fed him and told him to catch up on his sleep."

"So what was the message?" Blade asked the Family Leader.

Plato stretched and gazed at a group of children playing tag. "Evidently the Moles captured someone near their city. Wolfe suspected the man was spying and interrogated him. Unfortunately," Plato said, frowning, "this alleged spy did not survive the inter-rogation."

"Did he spill the beans before he kicked the bucket?" Hickok asked.

Plato glanced at the gunman. "Your colorful collo-quialisms never cease to astound me."

"Can you lay that on me again?" Hickok responded. "In plain English this time?"

"Forget that!" Blade said, a bit impatiently. As head Warrior, his paramount concern was the safety of the Family. And if Wolfe was alarmed enough to send a messenger, the message must be critical. "What was the rest of the runner's report?"

"The man the Moles caught would not divulge any details concerning his origin or his reason for being near the Mole city," Plato said, "but he did make a few per-plexing statements before he died."

"Like what?" Blade prompted.

"He gloated before he expired," Plato said. "He told Wolfe the Moles would all be dead before the year is done. He bragged that the Freedom Federation would be history, as he put it, before too long."

"How did he know about the Freedom Federation?" Blade asked.

"That's what bothered Wolfe," Plato stated. "That, and the equipment the man was carrying when appre-hended."

"What equipment?" Geronimo interjected.

Plato scanned the compound. "I sent Bertha after it." He spotted a dusky-hued woman approaching from the armory, A Block. "When I first saw you coming."

Bertha was another of the Family's Warriors, a member of Gamma Triad. She was remarkably lovely in a striking sort of way. Her features conveyed an abundance of inner strength and a supreme self-con-fidence. Curly black hair cascaded over her ears and down to her shirt collar. She wore tight-fitting fatigues and black boots. Her brown eyes lit up at the sight of Hickok. "Hey there, White Meat!" she cried out. "What's happening?"

"Not much," Hickok replied uneasily.

"Relax, sucker!" Bertha said, laughing. "I ain't gonna jump your buns in public!"

Hickok hooked his thumbs in his gunbelt and glared at her. "How many times do I gotta tell you to stop talking to me like that? I'm married, remember?"

Bertha chuckled and nudged him with her left elbow. "I can't help it if I think you're the best-lookin' hunk in the Home!"

Geronimo couldn't resist the opening. "If you think Hickok is the best-looking man here," he chimed in, "then I'd suggest you have your eyes examined by the Healers!"

"Bertha!" Blade snapped with a tone of authority in his voice.

Bertha straightened and faced the giant Warrior, her chief. "Yes, sir," she said, all seriousness.

"Everybody knows you still have a crush on Hickok," Blade said, "but now's not the time to indulge it." He pointed at the items in her right hand. "Are these what Plato sent you to get?"

Bertha nodded and extended her right arm. "Yes, sir. Here you go."

Blade took the two pieces of equipment, a square, black box and a futuristic rifle. "Thank you. That's all for now."

Bertha wheeled, puckered her lips in Hickok's direction, smirked, and walked off.

"You were a mite hard on her, weren't you?" Hickok commented.

"We're Warriors," Blade stated testily. "We're supposed to be disciplined. There's a time and a place for everything." He saw the others studying him, silent accusations in their eyes, and he averted his gaze. Hickok was right. He had been hard on Bertha. And he knew the reason why. The prospect of another threat to the Freedom Federation, to the Family and the Home, agitated him greatly. The past several months had been peaceful. He'd been able to relax, to enjoy life for a change. The last thing he wanted was another damn threat to the Family's security! The very idea angered him, and he'd foolishly vented his budding frustration on Bertha.

Dumb. Dumb. Dumb.

"These are what the spy was carrying?" Blade needlessly asked to distract the others.

"Yes," Plato confirmed. "Wolfe was quite upset by them."

Blade could readily understand Wolfe's motives. Both the rifle and the mysterious black box were in superb condition. Indeed, both appeared to be relatively new. But where did they come from? Who had the industrial capability, the manufacturing know-how and resources, to produce items of such superior quality? The shiny black box was outfitted with a row of knobs and control buttons positioned along the bottom of the top panel. Above the knobs was a glass plate covering a meter of some sort. A small, vented grill occupied the upper right corner. "What is this thing?"

Plato shrugged his skinny shoulders. "We don't know. The Elders have examined it, but we're unable to ascertain its function."

"Can I see that, pard?" Hickok inquired, reaching for the rifle.

Blade handed the gun over.

Hickok whistled in admiration as he hefted the firearm. "This is a right dandy piece of hardware," he said in appreciation. The entire gun, including the 20-inch barrel and the folding stock, was black to minimize any reflection. The barrel was tipped with a short silencer, and an elaborate scope was mounted above the ejection chamber. A 30-shot magazine protruded from under the rifle near the trigger guard. There were four buttons on one side of the gun, close to the stock, and a small, plastic panel above the buttons. On top of the scope was a fifth button, and extending from the front of the scope, at the top, was a four-inch tube or miniature barrel. "I never saw a gun like this," Hickok said, marveling, "and I know our gun books in the library like the palm of my hand."

Plato stroked his pointed chin, running his fingers through his beard. "Can you imagine the threat if an army, outfitted with a rifle like that one, laid siege to the Home?"

"We've fought off attackers before," Hickok

boasted.

"Yes," Plato concurred, "but they were ill-equipped. The rifle you're holding is of recent vintage. What if the same people responsible for that automatic rifle can also fabricate larger weaponry on an extensive scale? What then?"

Hickok didn't answer.

"We must find out where these came from," Blade announced.

"How?" Geronimo asked. "Wolfe killed the spy."

"We'll think of something," Blade said optimistically.

"We must keep this information amongst ourselves," Plato said. "There's no need to instill unnecessary anxiety in the Family."

"We'll keep quiet," Blade promised. "And I'll have a word with Bertha. Who else knows?"

"Ares," Plato revealed. "He was on guard duty on the west wall last night when the messenger arrived."

"Ares ain't exactly a blabbermouth," Hickok noted.

Ares was the head of Omega Triad and a superlative Warrior.

"But how will we find out where the spy came from?" Geronimo reiterated.

Blade opened his mouth to respond.

The hot air was abruptly rent by the strident blast of a horn sounding from the west rampart, the horn the Warriors used to signal in times of danger!

3

The 15 Family Warriors were armed with their favorite weapons and on the brick walls within three minutes of the alarm. Alpha Triad, consisting of Blade, Hickok, and Geronimo, took its posts on the west wall. They were joined by Beta Triad: the diminutive Rikki-Tikki-Tavi, the Family's supreme martial artist; the silver-haired Yama, named after the Hindu King of Death; and Teucer, the bowman. Gamma Triad took the north wall: Spartacus, with his ever-present broadsword; the eighteen-year-old Shane, an aspiring gunfighter like his mentor, Hickok; and Bertha. The east wall was manned by the towering, Mohawk-cropped Ares, the head of Omega Triad, and his two subordinates: Helen, a raven-haired Warrior whose namesake was Helen of Troy; and Sundance, the pistol expert. On the south wall stood Zulu Triad, led by the powerhouse Samson, and including Sherry, Hickok's wife, and Marcus, the self-styled gladiator. Sherry, her M.A.C.-10 held in the crook of her right arm, surveyed the empty field and forest below the wall, thankful little Ringo was being watched by Jenny, Blade's wife, and worried about her husband on the west wall.

Rikki-Tikki-Tavi had been responsible for blowing the horn. Now he was stationed alongside Blade directly above the closed drawbridge, his five-foot frame clothed in black Oriental-style clothing constructed by the Family Weavers, his dark eyes scanning the forest to the west. His attire matched his lineage. Rikki was one of several Family members with an Oriental lineage.

31

"So what's the big deal?" Hickok demanded, standing on Rikki's right. "There's nothin' out there."

"Be patient," Rikki advised.

For 150 yards in every direction, the Family diligently kept the land cleared of trees, brush, boulders, and whatever else might be used for concealment by any enemy assaulting the Home. The flat, exposed field gave the Warriors an excellent line of fire. No one could reach the brick walls without sustaining heavy casualties.

Beyond the fields, dense forest prevailed. A crude road, little more than a flattened 15-foot-wide path, was maintained between the western edge of the field and Highway 59, approximately five miles to the west. A mile south from where the makeshift road met Highway 59 was Halma, dwelling place of the Family's allies, the Clan.

"You sure you didn't see a deer and mistake it for a mutate?" Hickok asked, joking with Rikki.

Rikki pointed to the west. "Does that look like a deer to you?"

Hickok took a look. "Nope," he admitted. "It sure don't, pard."

A jeep was visible, cresting the rise of a low hill, heading toward the Home.

"It's about half a mile away," Geronimo commented.

The jeep was joined by two military troop transports and yet another jeep.

"It's a small convoy," Blade observed.

"The only ones we know with vehicles like those are the folks in the Civilized Zone," Hickok declared.

Blade nodded. Why would the Civilized Zone be sending a convoy to the Home? Even in military vehicles, the trip was fraught with peril and not to be taken lightly.

Someone cleared his throat to Blade's left.

The giant Warrior turned and discovered Plato had ascended the rampart. "What are you doing up here?" he demanded. "You shouldn't be up here until we signal it's all clear."

Plato smiled. "I wanted to see for myself. I know it's against our rules."

Hickok grinned. "You're settin' a fine example for the munchkins, old-timer."

"I promise I will leave at the first hint of hostility," Plato said to Blade.

Blade frowned. "All right. You can stay. But keep your head down!"

The convoy was rapidly closing on the Home. The leading jeep reached the field west of the compound and angled toward the drawbridge.

"Hold your fire!" Blade commanded. He held a Commando Arms Carbine in his hands. Converted to full automatic by the Family Gunsmiths, and outfitted with a 90-shot magazine for its 45-caliber ammunition, it was a particularly lethal instrument of death.

"Darn!" Hickok stated. "I was hoping for some target practice." He hefted the Navy Arms Henry Carbine in his right hand.

The other Warriors were likewise armed and ready. Geronimo carried an FNC Auto Rifle and packed an Arminius .357 Magnum in a shoulder holster under his right arm. Rikki-Tikki-Tavi had his cherished katana angled under his black belt, and held a Heckler and Koch HK93 in his arms. Rikki's Beta Triad companions were equally prepared: Teucer, the bowman, bore a Panther Crossbow, armed with explosive tips instead of razor-edged hunting points, the camouflage shading of the bow with a pull of 175 pounds complementing his green Robin Hood-like wardrobe; while Yama, one of the few Family members who could claim a physique nearly as superbly developed as Blade's, carried a variety of weapons. Yama was unique among the Warriors. He'd taken his name on his 16th birthday from the Hindu King of Death, not because he leaned toward the Hindu religion spiritually, but because death was his profession and he was an expert at his craft. At Yama's insistence, the Family Weavers had made a one-piece dark blue garment with the silhouette of a black skull stitched into the fabric between his wide shoulders to serve as his uniform. He normally used a Wilkinson

Carbine with a 50-shot magazine, a Browning Hi-Power 9-millimeter Automatic Pistol under his right arm, a Smith and Wesson Model 586 Distinguished Combat Magnum under his left arm, a 15-inch survival knife strapped to his right hip, and a curved scimitar in a scabbard on his left.

All of the weapons came from the Family armory in A Block. Kurt Carpenter had meticulously stockpiled hundreds of diverse arms in the huge, concrete structure. Rifles, pistols, revolvers, shotguns, machine guns, and others of every conceivable make and description. He also included at least one of each and every type of weapon he could find, everything from Oriental weaponry such as nunchaku and sai and to American Indian artifacts such as Apache tomahawks. Thus, the Warriors were able to satisfy their personal predilections, whether it was Bowies for Blade, a katana for Rikki, a broadsword for Spartacus (because Ares already possessed the only shortsword), or a tomahawk for Geronimo—the only remaining Family member with an Indian heritage. Whatever their tastes, the armory supplied them. Carpenter had predicted the collapse of civilization after the war, and he knew his successors would require considerable firepower if they were to persevere in a world governed by the basic creed of survival of the fittest.

The convoy stopped, the jeep ten yards from the west wall, and a figure in uniform emerged and glanced up at the Warriors.

Blade felt his muscles relax. The man was an officer, about six feet in height with a lean build. His uniform was clean and pressed, with gold insignia on his shoulders. He had black hair, brown eyes, and rugged, honest features. He was General Reese, the foremost military commander in the Civilized Zone under President Toland.

General Reese waved. "Blade! We need to talk!"

Blade returned the wave. "Hold on! We'll lower the drawbridge."

Four Family members quickly lowered the massive mechanism, and moments later the convoy wheeled into the compound and parked near the moat.

"Raise the drawbridge," Blade instructed Rikki. "And keep your Triad here until we find out what's going on."

"Will do," Rikki said.

"After you," Blade said to Plato, motioning toward the stairs. He waited until Plato was descending, then turned. "You two stay close to me," he said to Hickok and Geronimo. "I trust Reese, but you never know. . . ." He let the sentence trail off.

"Don't fret, pard," Hickok stated. "You can count on us. We'll back your play all the way."

Blade hastened after Plato, Hickok and Geronimo in tow.

General Reese had climbed from his jeep. A dozen soldiers piled from each of the troop transports, and four more from the second jeep. The troopers formed into two rows, standing at attention.

Blade saw a man and a woman step from the general's vehicle. They wore green uniforms similar to those worn by the Civilized Zone soldiers, but theirs were a darker green and the new fabric clung to their bodies. Both the man and the woman were well-proportioned, conveying considerable strength in their posture, in the muscular contours of their physiques, and in the alertness of their eyes. Both wore their black hair in crewcuts, and both had pistols strapped to their right hips. Professional military types, obviously, but there was something about them, perhaps in the simple way they carried themselves, serving to set them apart and above the troopers from the Civilized Zone. Neither the man's square features nor the woman's angular facial lines reflected any warmth or humor.

"Hello, General Reese," Blade said as they reached the vehicles. "It's good to see you again."

"Blade!" General Reese advanced and extended his right hand. "The same here!" He shook hands warmly, then faced Plato. "And you, sir, must be the Family Leader I've heard so much about. It is a pleasure to meet you at last."

Plato shook hands. "And I have heard about you.

President Toland informed me at our last conclave how instrumental you've been in assisting in the reorganization of the Civilized Zone government."

"President Toland flatters me," General Reese said.

Blade indicated his two friends. "This is Hickok."

"The famous gunfighter?" General Reese asked.

Hickok's chest puffed up a good inch. "I reckon my name does get bandied about a mite." He offered his right hand.

"You Warriors are acquiring quite a reputation," General Reese remarked.

"And this is Geronimo," Blade said.

General Reese shook hands. "We met briefly when you were in Denver, remember?"

"You have a good memory," Geronimo said.

"Well, now that the amenities are over," Plato stated, "perhaps you will explain the reason for this extraordinary visit?"

General Reese nodded at the man and woman in the dark green uniforms. "First let me introduce you."

The man and woman moved closer.

General Reese swept the Warriors and Plato with his gaze. "Gentlemen, I'd like you to meet Captain Wargo and Lieutenant Farrow."

Captain Wargo nodded. "I've looked forward to this meeting for some time." His voice was deep, almost harsh.

"They're from Chicago," General Reese revealed.

Plato's surprise showed. Hickok and Geronimo exchanged glances. Only Blade remained immobile, a statue.

"When did the Civilized Zone send an expedition to Chicago?" Plato inquired. "I thought such missions must be approved by the entire Freedom Federation Council?"

"We didn't send one," General Reese responded. "They came to us."

Blade studied the pair. Chicago was east of the area presided over by the Freedom Federation, in hostile country. No one had ventured to the Windy City in over a century. But during the last run Alpha Triad had made, to the city of St. Louis—during which they'd battled the Reds—he'd been told about a group controlling Chicago. What was its name again?

"We're Technics," Captain Wargo said proudly.

"Technics?" Plato repeated, puzzled.

"I believe it started as a nickname decades ago," Captain Wargo explained. "You see, the scientists at the Chicago Institute of Advanced Technology refused to evacuate the city during the war. They dug in and used their knowledge to forge a new lifestyle. Eventually they came to rule the city."

"And now they're known as Technics," Plato deduced.

"Exactly," Captain Wargo confirmed.

"They even have several manufacturing facilities operational," General Reese interjected.

"Really?" Plato's eyebrows rose. "Quite remarkable. The war severely impaired the country's industrial capability. How were your people able to overcome the handicap of a shortage of raw materials and the requisite work force to produce your goods?"

Captain Wargo shrugged, downplaying the Technics' accomplishment. "Oh, we get a little bit here, a little bit there. You know how it is."

Blade saw Hickok's jaw muscles tighten.

Plato nodded. "We must have a great deal to discuss. Why don't we retire to my cabin? My wife, Nadine, can fix refreshments, and you can elucidate on why you've been looking forward to meeting us."

"Sounds great," Captain Wargo said.

"I'll dismiss my men," General Reese declared, walking off.

"I'll join you in your cabin," Blade told Plato. Then he looked at Wargo. "If you don't mind?" he added politely.

"To the contrary," Captain Wargo replied. "I was hoping you would join us. And bring Hickok and Geronimo too. Alpha Triad should be there."

"You know who we are?" Blade asked innocently.

Captain Wargo hesitated for a fraction of an instant. "Yes. General Reese told me all about you on the trip here.''

Hickok's right hand had drifted to the pearl grips on his right Python.

Blade smiled. ''Plato, why don't you take Captain Wargo and Lieutenant Farrow to your cabin?'' he suggested. ''We'll join you in a bit.''

''Fine,'' Plato said, and led the Technics to the east.

''I don't trust that hombre,'' Hickok snapped when they were beyond earshot.

''Neither do I,'' Geronimo affirmed.

''That makes it unanimous,'' Blade said.

''What do you reckon they're up to?'' Hickok queried.

''We'll know shortly,'' Blade answered. He gazed up at the west rampart, at Rikki-Tikki-Tavi. ''The alert is over!'' he shouted. ''Tell the Family they can come out of the Blocks! Post Gamma Triad around these vehicles!''

''That won't be necessary,'' interrupted General Reese, joining them.

''Just a precaution,'' Blade said. ''Standard procedure.''

''Yeah,'' Hickok quipped. ''We wouldn't want one of our kids to steal a battery or a hubcap!''

''Have Omega Triad and Zulu Triad wait near the armory until they hear from me!'' Blade yelled to Rikki.

''Consider it done!'' Rikki acknowledged.

''Let's go,'' Blade said, and led them toward the row of cabins in the center of the Home. ''What do you make of this Captain Wargo?'' he inquired of the general.

Reese frowned. ''He's a real tough nut to crack. Doesn't talk a lot, except when it suits his purposes. To be honest, I don't feel comfortable around him. Or her, for that matter. I receive the impression they're holding back on us, not telling us everything they should.''

''You too, huh?'' Hickok said.

''President Toland feels the same,'' General Reese disclosed. ''He gave me a personal message for you, Blade.''

''What is it?''

"He said to watch yourself," General Reese stated. "Use your best judgment, but watch yourself."

"We will," Blade vowed. "What are they doing here?"

"You'd better hear it from them," General Reese said.

"Did they just show up in Denver?" Geronimo asked.

"No," General Reese responded. "They showed up at a guard post on the eastern edge of Omaha, Nebraska. Demanded to see President Toland. Asked for him by name."

"How did they know Toland is the President of the Civilized Zone?" Blade asked the officer.

"Beats me," General Reese said. "The word has probably spread, though, even to the Outlands."

"The Outlands?" Blade reiterated.

"Oh. Sorry. Anything beyond the boundaries of the Freedom Federation, whether it's west of the Rockies or east of our borders, we call the Outlands," General Reese informed them.

"Appropriate name," Geronimo chipped in.

"Did you interrogate this Wargo?" Blade asked.

"No," General Reese answered, frowning. "I wanted to give him the works, but President Toland wouldn't hear of it."

"Why not?"

"Because, technically, Captain Wargo and Lieutenant Farrow are diplomatic envoys for the Technics. They initiated peaceful overtures and established contact with us." He sighed. "My hands are tied until and unless they commit a hostile act."

"I can't wait to hear what these bozos have to say," Hickok commented.

They walked in silence to Plato's cabin, the seventh from the north. Blade knocked on the west door, and a moment later Plato opened it and beckoned them inside.

"Come on in," Plato urged them. "Nadine is in the kitchen preparing food for our guests. Would you like some, General Reese?"

Reese patted his stomach. "Thanks, but no thanks. I'm on a diet. I've got to lose about ten pounds. It doesn't do to set a bad example for the ranks."

"I heartily agree," said Captain Wargo. He was seated at the living room table. Lieutenant Farrow stood behind his chair, her hands clasped behind her trim back.

Plato closed the door and took a seat across the oaken table from Captain Wargo. General Reese sat on his left. Hickok and Geronimo moved to the right and leaned against the log wall. Blade crossed to the table, but stayed standing next to Plato.

"Have a seat," Captain Wargo suggested.

"Thanks," Blade said, "but not right now."

Captain Wargo shrugged.

"You were about to tell me the reason you wanted to meet us," Plato prompted the Technic officer.

Captain Wargo leaned back in his chair and stared at each of them, smiling.

There was a phony quality about that smile. Blade shifted uncomfortably.

"First, allow me to congratulate you on the marvelous setup you have here," Captain Wargo said. "It's amazing, considering the barbaric conditions existing elsewhere."

"Our Founder deserves all the credit," Plato said. "We're merely perpetuating a system he started."

Captain Wargo glanced at Blade. "And what about the Warriors? Did your Founder start them as well?"

"Originally he had nine Warriors, but later they were expanded to twelve, and then, fairly recently, to fifteen," Plato divulged.

"I couldn't help but notice," Captain Wargo remarked. "You have a Warrior named Hickok, and one called Geronimo, and others named Yama and Samson, to mention just a few." He paused. "Where do you people get your names? We have a vast library in Chicago, and a mandatory educational regimen. It seems to me I've run across some of these names before." He looked at Plato. "Especially yours."

Plato nodded, grinning. "The Family also has a

sizable library," he told Wargo. "And many of us take our names from books in the library."

"You get your names from books?"

"Our Founder didn't want us to forget our historical roots. He was afraid we'd be tempted to ignore the lessons to be learned from a study of history. So he implemented a procedure, a ceremony we call our Naming. When all Family members turn sixteen, they are permitted to select any name from any book in the library as their very own. Years ago, we only used the history books. But now we adopt our names from practically any volume in the library. That's how I received mine," Plato elaborated. "Hickok, for instance, took his from a revered gunfighter of ancient times. Geronimo took his from an Indian he admires and respects."

Captain Wargo looked at the giant Warrior alongside Plato. "And you, Blade?"

Blade patted his twin Bowies. "I couldn't find a name I wanted in any of the books, so I picked a new one."

"One based on his preference in weapons," Plato added.

"I see." Captain Wargo glanced at Lieutenant Farrow, then resumed speaking. "I don't mind telling you, and I'm not attempting to flatter you by saying this, that your reputations have preceded you. As General Reese noted earlier, you've achieved some small measure of fame over the past few years."

Blade studied the Technic. "I can understand them talking about us in the Civilized Zone," he said. "After all, we fought a war with them some time back and won. But how is it you've heard of us clear in Chicago? Chicago is outside of the Civilized Zone. It's even outside of the Freedom Federation's territory. It must be hundreds of miles from here."

"About eight hundred," Captain Wargo offered.

"Are you telling me you've heard of us in Chicago?" Blade demanded.

Captain Wargo nodded. "Think about it for a moment. From what I was told, the Warriors have fought in the Twin Cities, in Montana, in the Dakota

Territory, and in the Civilized Zone. You were responsible for destroying Cheyenne, Wyoming, too, I believe. Did you really think all that would go unnoticed?''

Blade thoughtfully chewed on his lower lip. Verrrry interesting! First, Wargo said he'd heard about the Warriors from General Reese. Now he says he learned about them in Chicago.

"General Reese only confirmed the stories," Captain Wargo said, as if he could read Blade's mind. "Chicago isn't isolated from the rest of the world. We get travelers passing through every day. We were bound to hear about you sooner or later.''

"I see," Blade said. Why was it he still felt as if Wargo were lying through his even white teeth?

"Actually," Captain Wargo said, "the Warriors are part of the reason I'm here.''

"They are?'' asked Plato.

"Yes," Captain Wargo confirmed. "The Warriors, and the SEAL.''

Blade's steely eyes bored into the Technic. The SEAL was the Family's mechanical pride and joy, their main means of travel. The Founder, Kurt Carpenter, had spent millions of dollars developing it prior to World War III. His scientists had been instructed to construct an indestructible vehicle, and they'd nearly succeeded. Van-like in configuration, the SEAL was green in color and designed with a versatile array of special features. It had originally been called the Solar-Energized Amphibious or Land Recreational Vehicle. Carpenter had later hired mercenaries to incorporate devastating armaments into its body. Its sturdy structure was composed of a shatterproof, heat-resistant, super-plastic, deliberately tinted to prevent outsiders from viewing the interior but enabling the occupants to see in all directions. Four enormous tires provided a rugged means of locomotion. Two prototypical solar panels on the roof and a series of six revolutionary batteries positioned in a lead-lined case under the SEAL served as the key components in its power system. "You know about the SEAL too?''

Captain Wargo nodded. "A little. We knew you owned it, and our leader, the man we call our Minister, realized you might be able to assist us in a desperate enterprise. We knew the Family was connected with the Freedom Federation, but we didn't know exactly where to find you. So the Minister proposed sending us to President Toland and requesting his aid in contacting you." Wargo grinned. "It worked."

"One moment," Plato said. "What is this desperate enterprise you've mentioned?"

Captain Wargo's grin widened. "Our Minister would like your permission to send Alpha Triad and your SEAL on a mission."

"A mission? To where?" Plato inquired.

Captain Wargo scanned the room before responding. "Why, to New York City, of course."

Blade felt his abdominal muscles inadvertently tighten.

4

The four soldiers in the jeep, three men and a woman, were five miles from the Home, hidden in the woods to the east of Highway 59.

"So what's the scoop, Sarge?" asked the woman trooper.

"We sit tight until we receive the signal," the sergeant advised her.

"This is boring," commented one of the men, seated in the back beside the woman.

The sergeant turned in his seat next to the driver. "You're a Technic, Johnson. I don't want to hear that kind of shit again!"

"Yes, sir, Sergeant Darden, sir," Private Johnson said. "My apology, sir."

Sergeant Darden stared at his subordinate for a minute, trying to determine if Johnson was being his typically sarcastic self.

"What's the name of these dumb hicks?" inquired the driver.

"They're called the Family," Sergeant Darden informed him.

"The Family?" The driver snickered. "What a corn-ball name!"

"Don't underestimate them," Sergeant Darden warned.

"Give us a break!" Johnson said. "You don't expect us to get worked up about a bunch of dirt farmers, do you?"

"They're not dirt farmers," Sergeant Darden responded. "Only about a dozen or so actually till the soil. The rest perform other duties. Besides, the ones you need to worry about are the Warriors."

"The Warriors?" Private Johnson snorted derisively. "Give us a break! How bad can they be?"

"The baddest," Sergeant Darden said.

"Says who?" demanded Johnson.

"Says the Minister," Sergeant Johnson stated.

"So why are we wasting these hicks?" asked the woman.

"Because those are our orders, Rundle," Sergeant Darden remarked.

"But why?" Rundle pressed him.

Sergeant Darden shrugged. "What's it matter? We do as we're told, no questions asked. You know that."

"Just wondered, is all," Rundle commented absently.

"We were lucky we received that warning about Halma," mentioned the driver. "Another mile and we'd of blundered right on 'em."

"Who were those people in that town?" asked Rundle.

"Don't know," Darden told her. "But I'd imagine they're friends of the Family's if they live so close to their Home."

"Say, Sarge," Private Johnson said. "What's with the beeper?"

Sergeant Darden studied the black box in his lap. "It's still stationary. They haven't moved."

"Do you think this Family will get wise to us?" asked Private Rundle.

"No way," Sergeant Darden declared.

Private Johnson yawned. "Who cares if they do or not? One way or the other, this Family is history!"

"Fine by me," said Rundle. "I could use some action."

5

"New York City?" Plato repeated in astonishment. "You can't be serious!"

"I've never been more serious," Captain Wargo declared.

Hickok laughed. "Who does this ding-a-ling think he is? He waltzes in here and tells us to go to New York City, just like that?" He snapped his fingers.

"I'm *asking* you, not telling you," Captain Wargo said with a touch of annoyance. "Or, rather, our Minister is asking you on behalf of all humanity."

"You'd better explain," Plato told the Technic.

"Certainly." Captain Wargo leaned forward. "You know what it's like out there in the world. It's a real jungle. Mutants everywhere. Roving bands of looters and killers. The few outposts of civilization don't stand much of a chance, do they?"

Plato didn't answer.

"There's no need for me to tell you how bad it is," Captain Wargo went on. "You know. Even in the area under the jurisdiction of your Freedom Federation, even in the Civilized Zone, it's not safe to be out alone after dark. I'd be willing to bet it's not even completely safe here in your Home. Am I right? Have any of the mutants ever managed to scale the walls and attack you?"

"We've experienced a few incidents," Plato conceded.

"See? What did I tell you?" Captain Wargo pounded

the table. "Don't you think it's about time all of that changed? Wouldn't you like to see the world the way it was? Peaceful? Prosperity for all?"

"This world has never known true peace," Plato said. "And in the prewar societies, only the rich knew prosperity."

"True. True," Captain Wargo said. "But you must admit it was safer for the general populace before the war than it is now."

"Perhaps," Plato allowed.

"Anyway," Captain Wargo continued. "You know as well as I do that everyone is barely scraping by today. There's never enough food or ample clothing or medical supplies."

"Do the Technics intend to remedy the shortages?" Plato asked.

"With your help," Captain Wargo replied.

"How?"

"Follow me on this," Captain Wargo said. "Before World War III, there was an eastern branch of the Institute of Advanced Technology—"

"Located in New York City?" Plato guessed.

"Exactly. Shortly before the war they succeeded in perfecting a new strain of seeds. Fruit and vegetable and grain seeds, radically different from anything seen before. These new seeds could grow in barren soil and required absolutely minimal amounts of water. They were designated the Genesis Seeds. Can you imagine what those seeds could do today? They would be a godsend! Farmers everywhere would be able to grow crops again in abundance! Starvation would disappear! Once we've reestablished the food supply, we can devote our attention to meeting other essential needs. It would be fantastic!" Captain Wargo stopped, his face flushed with excitement.

"And I take it you want Alpha Triad to travel to New York City and retrieve these Genesis Seeds?" Plato deduced.

"Precisely!" Captain Wargo answered.

Hickok laughed. "You're out of your gourd!"

Plato held up his right hand for silence. "This is a

very grave matter, and some clarification is needed. Let's consider your statements. You say these Genesis Seeds would deliver us from our agricultural bondage to a land contaminated and polluted by massive amounts of radiation and chemical toxins. Let us suppose for a moment these seeds really exist. Even if they are found, and they can do all you claim, they won't necessarily make the world a safer place in which to live."

"But it would be a start!" Captain Wargo said. "If we don't have to devote so much time and energy to food, we can channel them to our other problems like the mutants and the degenerates."

Plato pursed his thin lips. "The scenario you paint sounds encouraging. But look at the reality of your request. Wasn't New York City hit during World War III?"

"It was," Captain Wargo admitted. "We know the Soviets used thermonuclear devices sparingly during the war, apparently with the intent of conquering the U.S. instead of wiping us off the face of the earth. They preferred to use neutron bombs and missiles on most of the populated centers they struck. But New York and a few others were exceptions. New York was hit by a hydrogen-tipped ICBM."

"We understand the Soviets still control some of the country," Plato mentioned.

"True. They occupy a belt in the eastern U.S., but New York City is not included in the area they control," Captain Wargo said.

"So getting back to New York City," Plato stated, "how do we justify sending our Warriors into a contaminated zone, into a potential hot spot?"

"New York isn't hot anymore," Captain Wargo said.

"You've verified that fact?" Plato demanded.

Captain Wargo nodded. "Let me explain." He paused. "You said you're familiar with prewar history?"

"Extensively," Plato affirmed.

"Good. Then you must know about the two Japanese cities hit by nuclear weapons during World War II, way, way back in the 1940s. I think their names were Hiroshima and Nagasaki.''

"They were," Plato declared.

"Like Hiroshima and Nagasaki, New York City was hit by an airburst of incredible magnitude. It obliterated a huge area and razed most of the buildings within a twenty-five-mile radius. But because it was an airburst, the fallout was minimal.''

"Why was that?" General Reese interrupted.

"Fallout," Captain Wargo elaborated, "is produced when a nuclear explosion takes place on the ground. The blast sucks up tons and tons of dirt and carries it into the atmosphere. All of this dirt then becomes radio-active, and when it falls back to the ground you get your fallout. But in an airburst, because the blast takes place up in the sky, no dirt is sucked up, and without the dirt there's nothing to fall back down. So no fallout." He cleared his throat. "Hiroshima and Nagasaki were hit, all right, but within thirty years of the strike you would have been hard-pressed to find any trace of the explosions. Both cities were densely populated. Both had lush landscaping and many flowering gardens. And if Hiroshima and Nagasaki were completely safe a few decades after the nuclear bombs were dropped, then New York City, from a radiation-contamination stand-point, is safe by now.''

"Hmmmm," Plato said, reflecting.

"So you won't need to worry about your Warriors getting radiation poisoning," Captain Wargo told the Family Leader.

"Then let's tackle another issue," Plato said. "What makes you think the Genesis Seeds are still there?"

Captain Wargo smiled. "Because we know the building the seeds were stored in is still there."

"How do you know this?" Plato inquired.

The Technic frowned and gazed at the wooden floor. "We've already tried to retrieve the Genesis Seeds."

"You have?" Plato asked in surprise.

"Yes. We've sent in a few teams—"

"How many?" Plato broke in.

"I can't remember, offhand," Captain Wargo said. "A few."

"What happened to them?" Blade queried.

Captain Wargo sighed. "They failed. The first squad didn't even make it to the site of the building. The New York branch of the Institute of Advanced Technology was destroyed in the blast, all of it except for the lower levels. And the Genesis Seeds were placed in a vault deep underground. That's another reason we feel the Genesis Seeds are still there."

"What happened to your other teams?" Blade asked.

"The second squad reached the site and radioed they were going underground," Captain Wargo answered. "That's the last we heard from them."

"No idea what happened to 'em, huh?" Hickok chimed in.

Captain Wargo's thin lips twitched. "Oh, we have an idea. In fact, we know what probably got them. The Zombies."

Plato straightened in his chair. "The Zombies?"

Captain Wargo's eyes seemed to glaze slightly, and there was a hint of horror in his voice. "New York City is inhabited. We think a lot of the poor slobs stayed on after the war, not having anywhere else to go. They undoubtedly took to the sewers, the subways, and whatever other underground tunnels existed. Over the years the radiation took its toll on their bodies, on their genes—"

"But I thought you said there wasn't any fallout," Blade interjected.

"No radioactive fallout," Captain Wargo said. "But there still was some radioactivity, enough to produce the inevitable mutations. And those mutations now roam New York City at will, killing every living thing they encounter."

Blade felt a shiver run up his spine. He found himself fervently hoping Plato would decline the Technics' request.

"You call these mutations Zombies?" Plato asked.

Captain Wargo nodded. "Yes. Our last two teams

were able to penetrate the lower levels, but none of them came out alive. The Zombies ate them.''

"Ate them?'' This came from Geronimo, his tone shocked.

Captain Wargo looked up. "Oh? Didn't I tell you? The Zombies are cannibals.''

There was a moment of strained silence.

"What makes you think our Warriors would fare any better than the teams you sent in?'' Plato demanded.

Captain Wargo brightened. "Your SEAL. You see, we do have a manufacturing capability, and we can produce some rather sophisticated weapons, but nothing on a large scale. No tanks, nothing like that. And even if we could manufacture a tank, where would we obtain the fuel to operate it? And without a tank, or a similar vehicle, there's no way to guarantee our squads can reach the site in one piece. But with this SEAL I've heard tell about, we could get our people there intact. Then, all they'd need do is make it to the underground vault and retrieve the Seed canisters.''

"Is that all?'' Hickok chuckled.

Blade ran his right hand along the cool hilt of his right Bowie. Wargo was lying again. He was sure of it. His mind flashed to his run to St. Louis, and he remembered being told interesting information concerning the Technics: they ruled Chicago, they were technologically superior to anybody else, and they had formed a pact with the bikers running St. Louis. One provision of the pact called for the Technics to supply the bikers, known as the Leather Knights, with unlimited amounts of fuel for their bikes. And if the Technics could provide vast quantities of fuel to the bikers, then they also had enough to fuel a tank. Or a dozen tanks.

So what the hell was Captain Wargo up to?

"Our proposal is this,'' Capain Wargo said. "Our Minister would like your Alpha Triad to transport a retrieval squad to New York City. In exchange, we will share the Genesis Seeds with you.''

"Share them?'' Plato repeated.

"Yes. Our Minister will give your Family half of all

the Seeds recovered. You can do with them whatever you like. Keep them for yourselves, or share them with your allies in the Freedom Federation.''

"Your Minister is most . . . generous," Plato said.

"If the Genesis Seeds are recovered, we can afford to be," Captain Wargo remarked. "We won't need all of them. If you ask me, it's a pretty good deal."

"The Elders will discuss it," Plato told him.

"Fine by me." He rested his elbows on the table, then glanced behind him as if suddenly recalling something important.

Lieutenant Farrow was still behind his chair.

"I almost forgot," Captain Wargo said, facing Plato. "Our Minister wanted to prove his honorable intentions. He thought you might not trust us, or wouldn't believe our offer. So he authorized me to present a token of his sincerity."

"What sort of token?" Plato inquired.

"Lieutenant Farrow."

Plato's brow furrowed. "I don't understand."

Captain Wargo spread his hands on the table. "It's simple. Lieutenant Farrow will be our insurance."

Plato stared at the woman officer. "I don't see how—"

"Lieutenant Farrow will be your hostage," Captain Wargo detailed. "The proof of our performance, as it were."

"Our hostage?" Plato and Blade exchanged glances.

"Sure. She stays here until your Warriors return. We're putting her life in your hands as an example of our good intentions. If your Warriors don't return, kill her," Captain Wargo stated matter-of-factly.

"You can't be serious," Plato countered in amazement.

"Very serious," Captain Wargo said. "Our Minister is a man of his word, and this is his way of demonstrating the fact."

Plato opened his mouth to speak, then thought better of the idea. He glanced up at Blade, his face expressionless except for his eyes. Smoldering contempt flashed briefly, then vanished as he gazed at the Technics. "And how does Lieutenant Farrow feel about this hostage business?''

Captain Wargo looked at Farrow. "Tell him," he ordered.

"I am a Technic," Lieutenant Farrow dutifully intoned. "I do my duty."

"I see." Plato stared at the table for a minute. "This has been most interesting," he said at last. "I must discuss your offer with Alpha Triad and the Family Elders. In private."

"I understand," Captain Wargo said. "Would you mind if we took a tour of your Home in the meantime?''

"Be my guest," Plato said.

"We'll supply a guide for you," Blade quickly added.

Captain Wargo stood. "That won't be necessary."

"We don't mind," Blade informed him.

"But we don't want to impose—" Captain Wargo began.

"It's no imposition," Blade said, cutting him off. He glanced at General Reese. "Would you escort our guests to the west wall?"

"Certainly," General Reese replied.

"Relay a message to Rikki for me," Blade directed. "Tell him to have Yama conduct Captain Wargo and Lieutenant Farrow on a tour of the Home."

"Will do," General Reese said. He motioned toward the cabin door.

"I almost forgot!" Plato abruptly exclaimed. "What about your refreshments?"

"We can eat later," Captain Wargo said.

"As you wish," Plato commented.

General Reese, Captain Wargo, and Lieutenant Farrow departed the cabin.

"Your reactions?" Plato immediately asked.

"White man speak with forked tongue," Geronimo said somberly, then grinned. "But what else is new?"

"My nose was twitching the whole time he was yappin'," Hickok declared.

"Your nose was twitching?" Plato reiterated.

"Yep. That dude reeked of unadulterated manure!" Hickok stated.

"And if anyone knows about manure," Geronimo said, "it's Hickok." His face suddenly displayed deep shock, and he gaped at the gunman. "Did I hear you right? Unadulterated? Have you been reading the dictionary again?"

"And your assessment?" Plato asked Blade.

Blade shook his head. "I don't trust these Technics one bit. When we were in St. Louis I discovered a few facts concerning them."

"On the run the Chronicler refers to as the Capital Run?" Plato said.

"That one. Captain Wargo was lying to us. From what I learned, the Technics could easily fuel a whole squadron of tanks. And what about those other sophisticated weapons he mentioned? So why do they need the SEAL?"

"Mystery number one," Plato said.

"And do you really believe the Genesis Seeds exist? Even if they do, why should the Technics generously share them with us?" Blade inquired.

"Mystery number two," Plato said.

"And how do they know so much about us?" Blade went on. "Granted, they might have learned a lot while in the Civilized Zone. But they obviously knew about us before they showed up in Omaha. Did they really hear about us from passing travelers in Chicago?"

"Mystery number three," Plato said.

"And who is this Minister? How does he fit into the scheme of things?"

"Mystery number four," Plato said, waiting for Blade to continue. When the huge Warrior stayed quiet, he surveyed the three members of Alpha Triad. "You've each broached salient points," he said, "but you've failed to stress the most perplexing mystery of all."

"What's that?" Hickok queried.

"Specifically, what type of individual offers one of his own people as a hostage, as a token, as a sacrifice, treating her life as callously as you or I might regard a mere fly?" Plato asked them.

"He must not think too highly of her," Geronimo speculated.

"Or he thinks too highly of himself," Plato opined. "Either way, I received the distinct impression this Minister is a calculating, cold-blooded person. I don't trust their offer either."

Blade breathed a silent sigh of relief. "Then you'll recommend to the Elders we reject their proposal?"

"On the contrary," Plato responded. "I will recommend we accept the Technics' offer."

"But you just said you don't trust them," Blade exclaimed.

"I don't," Plato admitted. "Which is precisely the reason we should take them up on it." He saw the looks of confusion on the trio of Warriors. "My rationale is simple. If these Technics have concocted some sort of devious design, if they pose a threat to our Family and our Home, then it is up to us to ascertain the nature of their threat and eliminate it as speedily as possible. We could attempt to force the information from Wargo and Farrow, but they might not cooperate. Indeed, they might be unaware of the Minister's plans. So what does that leave us? Only one recourse. We must, as they say, play along with them until we can discover their true motives and, if necessary, thwart any hostile maneuvers." He paused. "You can see I'm right, can't you?"

"Sounds peachy to me," Hickok commented.

"I agree with you," Geronimo said.

Blade hesitated. He definitely didn't want to go on another run. Sooner or later, the odds would catch up with him and Jenny would find herself a widow. Still, as head Warrior, his primary responsibility was to the Family. If the Technics were a menace, then they must be eliminated. He sighed. "I agree too."

"Good." Plato smiled. "I will call a gathering of the Elders and we'll discuss the situation. I'm positive they will concur with my conclusions."

Hickok happened to glance in the direction of the kitchen doorway. He straightened and placed a finger over his lips.

Everyone turned.

Plato's wife, Nadine, was framed in the doorway, a tray of sizzling venison soup in her frail hands. Her hair was gray, her eyes a compassionate brown, her face wrinkled and conveying a sense of noble character. She wore a blue denim dress, sewn together from the remains of a dozen pair of jeans. Her eyes were watering. "Is there no end to the violence?" she asked her husband.

"How long were you standing there?" Plato inquired.

"Long enough," Nadine said. "Must you send Alpha Triad out again?"

"How else can we learn the Technics' true motives?" Plato responded.

"There must be another way."

"If you know of one," Plato told her, "I'm open to suggestions."

Nadine stared at the Warriors. "I feel so sorry for them. They are always going off somewhere or another, fighting for their lives. What about their families? What about their children? Don't they have the right to a peaceful life like the rest of us?"

"They're Warriors," Plato said gravely. "No one compelled them to take their oath of allegiance, and they can resign whenever they want." He twisted. "Do any of you want out?"

"Not me, old-timer," Hickok said. "I've always had a secret hankerin' to see the Rotten Apple."

"That's the Big Apple," Geronimo corrected him. "And where they go, I go. Someone has to babysit Hickok."

"And what about you?" Plato asked Blade.

There was only one possible answer. Blade knew it, although he balked at voicing the words. Plato had hit the nail on the head. No one had twisted his arm to become a Warrior. He'd chosen his profession because he firmly believed the Family's safety and survival were of paramount importance. If the Technics were a threat to the Family, then, as Plato had said, the threat must be removed. "Alpha Triad is a team," Blade said to Plato. "One for all, and all for one."

"Now where have we heard that before?" Geronimo inquired, grinning.

"Then it's settled," Plato announced. "I will convene a special meeting of the Elders. If all goes as expected, you should be able to leave by this time tomorrow."

"I can hardly wait!" Hickok said enthusiastically.

Blade balled his huge hands into massive fists. There was no escaping his destiny. As head Warrior, he *had* to go.

"Let's have a quick bowl of soup first," Plato proposed.

Hickok walked to the table and pulled out a chair. "Sounds good to me. I'm so hungry, I could eat a horse!"

"You're always hungry," Geronimo commented.

Nadine carefully placed the metal tray on the living room table. "Enjoy yourselves!" she advised them.

Hickok studied Blade. "Don't get uptight, pard," he said. "This will be a piece of cake!"

"You wish!" Geronimo rejoined. "We'll be fortunate if we come back alive."

Hickok leaned toward Blade. "Maybe we should leave Geronimo here this time," he suggested.

"Why's that?" Blade asked.

The gunman frowned. "I don't rightly know if I can take much more of his rosy disposition."

6

Lieutenant Alicia Farrow was impressed, and it took a lot to impress her. As a combat-tested veteran with seven years in the Technic Elite Service, the commando arm of the Technic Army, she'd seen countless soldiers over the years. She'd fought side by side with some of the toughest men and women around. So she wasn't about to be awed by other professional fighters, not unless they were exceptional.

The Warriors were exceptional.

She'd observed their training sessions: their marksmanship practice on the firing range in the southeast corner of the Home, their martial-arts tutelage under the direction of a stately Elder, and their individualized workouts with their favorite weapons. Over the past three days, she'd developed an abiding respect for the Warriors. She found herself, despite her better judgment, admiring their inherent integrity and devotion to the Family.

It was too bad they had to die.

But the Minister had been most explicit. The Warriors, even the entire Family, must be eradicated. If the Technics were to assume their rightful place as world rulers, then every potential rival must be destroyed. The Freedom Federation was too large to be overcome in one fell swoop. Accordingly, the Minister had decided to selectively smash the separate Freedom Federation members beginning with the Family. His reasoning was logical and sound. Although the Family was the smallest contingent in the Freedom Federation numerically speaking, it exerted the controlling influence in the Federation's periodic Councils. The Family was becoming a symbol, a beacon of hope in a land ravaged by nuclear and chemical devastation. Wargo had told Plato the truth. Stories were spreading about the Family and the Warriors, and not just in the Freedom Federation but in the Outlands beyond. In an age when written and electronic communications and records were virtually nonexistent, fireside tales were the order of the day. Families would gather about their hearths at night, singles would congregate at crude "watering holes" where rotgut beverages were served, and in towns and settlements throughout the land everyone would exchange the latest information, the newest gossip they might have heard from a passing traveler. Serving as both a means of public dissemination of knowledge and a popular socializing entertainment, the stories grew as they were conveyed from mouth to mouth, from one inhabited outpost to the next. To some, the Home was becoming a sort of modern Utopia, while several of the Warriors had acquired mythical proportions. Ages prior, a Greek named Homer had regaled his listeners by extolling the herculean exploits of Achilles, Odysseus, Telamonian Aias, Diomedes and company. Now the cycle was being repeated, and the Minister did not like it one bit.

The Technics were determined to crush all potential opposition and assert their natural superiority. As long as the Family existed, the people had a source of inspiration and encouragement. If the Family fell, so would the hopes and aspirations of thousands, making the conquest of America easier. The Freedom Federation would become demoralized if the Family perished, and they might even disband without the Family's unifying persuasiveness to guide them.

As she stood near A Block, watching Rikki-Tikki-Tavi and Yama spar, Lieutenant Farrow reviewed the Minister's plan and marveled at his brilliance. The Family could be wiped out with a small force, the Minister had stated, his black eyes blazing at her from his elevated dais in the Technic throne room. The first step would be to gain their trust. The second to lure several of the Warriors and the SEAL away from the Home. And the final step would take place when the signal was given for the demolition team to level the Home, a demolition team of four commandos waiting in the forest outside the walls.

A signal Lieutenant Farrow had to give.

Farrow observed the flowing swirl of motion as Rikki and Yama engaged again, their arms and legs whirling, their martial-arts techniques honed to perfection.

Despite his diminutive stature, Rikki was more than holding his own. His black form pranced around the big man in blue, flicking hand and foot blows with precise control. For his part, Yama was hard-pressed to prevent any of Rikki's bone-shattering strikes from connecting. After several minutes of sustained mock combat, Rikki abruptly stepped back and bowed to his opponent, a grin creasing his face.

"You are improving," Rikki said.

Yama bowed and smiled. "Coming from you, that's a real compliment."

"Same time tomorrow?" Rikki asked, wiping his right palm across his perspiring brow.

"Fine by me," Yama replied.

Rikki glanced toward the Technic officer, ten yards away, his brown eyes narrowing. "She follows you everywhere, doesn't she?"

Yama nodded. "I've been appointed as her official Family liaison."

"I'm sure that's the reason she sticks by your side," Rikki remarked, his white teeth flashing.

"Are you trying to imply something?" Yama inquired. He ran his left hand through his fine, silver hair and stroked his drooping silver mustache.

"Not me," Rikki responded innocently. "But you should thank the Spirit Hickok isn't here."

"Why?"

"You know Hickok," Rikki said, still grinning. "He likes to tease everyone."

"But you don't?" Yama asked.

Rikki chuckled. "Of course not. A disciplined martial

artist does not demean himself by exhibiting crude humor.''

Yama laughed. ''If you ask me, you've been hanging around Geronimo too much.''

''Why do you say that?''

''Because you're starting to sling as much bull as he does,'' Yama said, and the two Warriors laughed together.

Lieutenant Farrow moved toward them. ''May I compliment both of you on your skill?''

Rikki bowed slightly. ''Thank you.''

''Are all of the Warriors as proficient as you?'' Farrow inquired.

''All of the Warriors are skilled,'' Rikki answered.

''He's too modest,'' Yama interjected. ''Rikki is the best martial artist in the Family.''

''From what I saw,'' Lieutenant Farrow said, ''you're as good as he is.''

Rikki grinned at Yama. ''I have duties to attend to. I'll see you later.'' His katana was leaning against a maple tree ten feet away to their right, next to Yama's usual arsenal. He walked over and reclaimed his sword, slid it through his belt, and headed toward B Block.

''Did I offend him?'' Lieutenant Farrow asked, her brown eyes probing Yama's blue.

''No,'' Yama told her. ''He thought we might like to be alone.''

''Why in the world would he think that?'' Farrow demanded defensively.

Yama shrugged and walked to the maple tree. He replaced the Browning Hi-Power 9-millimeter Automatic Pistol under his right arm, and slid the Smith and Wesson Model 586 Distinguished Combat Magnum into his left shoulder holster. The 15-inch survival knife was returned to its sheath on his right hip, and the gleaming scimitar took its customary position on his left hip. Finally, he picked the Wilkinson Carbine up from the green grass, wiped the barrel, and slung the gun over his left shoulder.

''Do you always pack so much hardware?'' Farrow asked.

"Always," Yama replied.

"Why?" she wanted to know.

"The more diverse my arms, the more effective I can be," Yama explained.

"I get the impression you're very, very effective," Farrow said.

Yama was about to reply when a terrified scream rent the air.

"What was that?" Farrow questioned him, looking around.

Yama was already moving, heading in the direction of the drawbridge at a rapid clip.

Lieutenant Farrow hurried after him. "What is it?" she cried.

Yama didn't bother to respond. He ran faster as a second scream wafted over the compound, coming from the west, from the field beyond the west wall. The drawbridge was down, and he knew several Family members were in the field, working at removing a cluster of weeds growing about 40 yards from the wall. Normally a tedious routine, the clearing detail could be fraught with danger because of the proximity to the forest. Once a week three Tillers went outside the walls to attend to the clearing, guarded by the Warriors on the ramparts. Seldom did the Tillers encounter trouble so close to the Home, and never had the Warriors failed to protect them.

This day was different.

As Yama reached the bridge over the moat he glanced up and spotted Ares on the rampart directly above. At six feet, three inches in height, lean and all muscle, Ares was a formidable Warrior, but he accented his fierceness by shaving the hair on both sides of his head and leaving a trimmed, red crest from his forehead to his spine. He wore dark brown leather breeches, a matching shirt, and sandals, and carried a short sword on his left hip. Yama saw Ares furiously tugging on the magazine in his automatic rifle.

Ares saw Yama crossing the bridge. "The damn thing's jammed!" he yelled in frustration. "Hurry!"

Other Family members were hastening toward the

bridge.

Yama was the first across the drawbridge. He took in the tableau before him and darted toward the Tillers.

They desperately needed help.

Any help.

One of the Tillers, an elderly man, was already down, his chest torn to bloody ribbons. Two other Tillers, a youth and an attractive blonde woman, both wearing green overalls, were eight feet off, both seemingly riveted in place, frozen by the sight of their attackers.

Because there were two of them.

Once they might have been called gray wolves. Now they were deformed mutations, their very genes corrupted and transformed by the poisons in the environment. Born disfigured, these two had survived their infancy and struck off together to rear more mutations like themselves.

Accustomed as he was to the sight of mutations and the even worse mutates, Yama nevertheless repressed a shudder as he closed on the deviate duo.

Both wolves were over five feet at the shoulder. Both were covered with a coat of gray fur. But after that, any resemblance to a real wolf was strictly coincidental. Each had six legs instead of four, and each leg was tipped with tapering talons instead of paws. By a curious genetic quirk, both creatures had two tails and, incredibly, two heads. The second head extended from the front of each mutant's neck. It was somewhat smaller than the original head, but its mouth was equally filled with a glistening array of pointed teeth. Red, baleful eyes were fastened on the Tillers. Both were slavering and growling, standing side by side next to the dead man sprawled before them.

Yama never hesitated.

The wolves were 30 yards away when he unslung his Wilkinson and aimed into the air. The two Tillers still alive were between the wolves and him, and Yama didn't want to risk accidentally winging one of them. He elevated the Wilkinson barrel and fired a short burst into the air.

Neither wolf so much as flinched.

The mutants shifted their attention to the approaching man in blue. Four heads raised skyward, and four husky throats bayed their defiant challenge. They bounded forward, separating, one to the right and the other to the left, temporarily forgetting the two Tillers as they concentrated on the human in blue.

"Get down!" Yama shouted to the Tillers.

They didn't budge, gaping at their fallen companion.

Yama angled to the left, wanting a clear line of fire. He dropped to his right knee, raised the Wilkinson, and fired.

The mutant on the left was caught in mid-stride. It was knocked onto its side by the impact of the heavy slugs and lay still.

Yama shifted to cover the other wolf.

The first one sprang to its feet and resumed its charge.

Yama waited for the second wolf to get closer, his finger on the trigger of the Wilkinson. Focused on the second wolf, he mistakenly neglected to verify the first was dead.

The oversight cost him.

Yama was squeezing the trigger to fire at the second mutant, when someone behind him shrieked a warning.

"Yama! Look out!"

Yama swiveled, too late. He glimpsed a heavy body and a lot of fur, and then something slammed into his chest, sending the Wilkinson flying, and he landed on his broad back with the first wolf straddling his legs and snarling.

The second wolf was 15 yards distant and bounding toward its mate.

Yama tensed, his hands at his sides, waiting for the mutant to make a move. He knew if he so much as twitched, the wolf would be on him ripping and tearing with its strong teeth and talons. He didn't want to do anything to provoke it. He was tempted to grab his survival knife, but realized the consequences.

The mutant inched toward its prey's neck, puzzled by the human's inexplicable immobility.

A pistol cracked, four times in swift succession.

Yama saw the bullets hit the wolf straddling him. He

could see the thing jerk as the shots hit home.

Who was doing the shooting? Ares?

The wolf growled and leaped to the attack, vaulting over the prone Warrior after this new assailant.

Yama rolled to his feet, drawing his scimitar. His blue eyes widened when he found his benefactor. It wasn't Ares or one of the other Warriors.

It was Lieutenant Farrow.

The Technic officer was holding her automatic pistol in her right hand and using her left hand to brace her right wrist. Her legs spread wide, her left eye closed, she aimed and fired again.

The nearest mutant twisted, blood spurting from its ruptured throat, but it kept coming, saliva dripping from its lower jaws.

Lieutenant Farrow blasted the wolf two more times.

Yama raced after the mutants. They were almost upon Farrow, and her shots weren't having any apparent affect.

Farrow fired twice more, then her pistol clicked on empty.

Yama was too far away to lend her assistance.

The first mutant leaped for Farrow's jugular.

The Technic dodged to the right, narrowly evading the slashing talons of the genetic deviate. She turned, keeping her eyes on the first wolf, inadvertently exposing her back to the second.

Yama was ten feet off, still too far away to be of any use. Unless he could distract the mutants. "Try me!" he shouted savagely. "Me!"

The second wolf, bounding between Yama and the Technic, abruptly spun at the sound of the harsh voice to its rear. Its fiery eyes alighted on the Warrior in blue, and it charged.

Yama stopped, holding his scimitar at chest height, waiting, gathering his strength. If he missed, the mutant wouldn't give him a second chance.

The wolf was on him in a gray streak, its jaws snapping at his waist and legs, snarling ferociously.

Yama's bulging muscles powered the scimitar in a vicious arc, the curved sword gleaming in the bright sunlight as it whisked through the air and into the springing mutant, connecting, slicing into the creature's top head, into its forehead, neatly severing a section of the wolf's scalp in a spray of crimson, hair, and flesh.

The wolf went down in a disjointed heap.

Yama knew the thing was still alive, but he couldn't waste a precious second.

The first mutant had Farrow on the ground, its lower jaw locked on her left forearm, and was brutally wrenching her from side to side while its top head attempted to bite her neck.

Yama reached them in four strides. The scimitar drove up and down in a shining glitter of light, the razor edge entering the wolf behind its upper ears and penetrating six inches into its skull.

The mutant stiffened, released Farrow, and spasmodically tore to the right, away from the man in blue. The force of its momentum yanked the scimitar from Yama's hands. It staggered from the wound, its upper eyes glazing over but its lower orbs alert and enraged.

Yama reached down and hauled Farrow erect. Her left forearm was bleeding profusely, and her features were pale, although she tried to muster a reassuring grin.

Yama reached for his Browning, but even as he did Farrow pointed over his right shoulder and started to scream a warning. He turned, the Browning coming clear of its holster.

The second wolf, the one with the missing scalp, was nearly on them, eight feet distant and sweeping forward.

A small figure in black suddenly hurtled past Yama and Farrow, a katana gripped in both hands, darting toward the raging mutant. Without hesitating, without missing a beat, Rikki-Tikk-Tavi assumed the horse stance, squatted, and swung his katana with the blade close to the ground.

Surprised by the appearance of another foe, dazed from the blow Yama had inflicted, the second wolf was unable to react in time. It felt a searing pain in all six legs as its lower limbs were hacked from its body. It instantly collapsed, its means of locomotion gone, and landed on its stomach. The mutant endeavored to flip onto its left side, to evade the human in black.

It failed.

Rikki reared over the second wolf, the katana held aloft, and slashed once, twice, three times, each stroke splitting the mutant's body further, almost severing the twin heads from its bulky form.

Yama, fascinated by Rikki's skilled dispatching of the second wolf, suddenly remembered the first mutant and turned.

The scimitar imbedded in its top head, the first wolf lurched at the man in blue and the injured woman.

A lanky shape dressed in brown ran into view behind the first mutant, his red Mohawk bobbing as he jogged nearer, his face a study in primal fury. "Get out of the way!" he bellowed.

Yama looped his left arm around Farrow's trim waist and leaped, drawing her with him, dropping to the ground and flattening, glancing over his right shoulder and seeing Rikki performing a similar maneuver.

And then Ares was there. Perhaps it was his red hair, maybe his inherited temperament, but Ares was known as the most hotheaded Warrior. He had once escorted two Healers outside of the Home, protecting them while they searched for herbs. The Healers had stumbled across a large black bear, and the bear attacked. Ares came to their rescue. According to the Healers, the bear never stood a chance. Ares took it on with just his short sword and made mincemeat of the hapless predator. The Healers later stated Ares seemed to be enjoying himself as he fought. Too much. So whether justified or not, Ares was considered to be particularly bloodthirsty when his wrath was aroused.

And at the moment he was incensed beyond endurance.

Irritated by the jamming of his gun, inflamed by the death of the Tiller while under his guard, and racked by a tormenting sense of personal guilt, he had cleared his weapon and raced to aid Yama and Rikki. Now, his face contorted, his features livid, he raised his automatic rifle and fired at the first mutant, his slugs stitching across its heads and abdomen, and he fired as it stumbled and fell onto its knees, fired as it desperately tried to stand and lunge at him, and fired until both heads were a mass of shattered reddish pulp. Not content with the death of the first mutant, Ares advanced on the second. Although the wolf was limp, its eyes lifeless, its body flat on the ground, the Mohawk-topped Warrior slowly walked toward it, pumping round after round into the mutant, and only suspending his one-man barrage when the rifle lacked bullets to shoot.

Ares stood next to the decimated mutant, sweat coating his hawkish face, and kicked it.

"I think it's dead," Rikki remarked, standing.

Yama stood, helping Farrow to rise.

Ares gazed at the deceased Tiller. He turned to Rikki, his green eyes rimmed with moisture. "I killed him," he said in a subdued tone.

"You did not kill him," Rikki said, disputing Ares. "I was inside B Block when this began and I didn't hear the initial screams. One of the others told me about them, and I saw you working with your gun as I was running toward the drawbridge. Guns jam. It's a fact of life."

"I killed him," Ares asserted forlornly.

Rikki walked over to Ares and placed his right hand on Ares's left arm. "You did not kill him, my brother. Don't blame yourself."

Ares stared at the Tiller again. "Dear Spirit!" he said.

Other Warriors and Family members were emerging from the Home.

"We can talk about this later," Rikki offered.

Ares looked down at Rikki. "I want a Review."

"You what?" Rikki responded in surprise.

"I want an official Warrior Review Board to call a hearing and rule on my actions," Ares stated.

Rikki glanced at Yama, who frowned. "This isn't necessary," he told Ares.

"It is for me," Ares countered. "I demand a Review

Board, and as a Warrior it's my right to have one.''

"But Blade is absent," Rikki said. "He usually heads the Review Boards.''

"Don't stall," Ares responded. "Blade doesn't need to be here for a Review Board to be held. Besides, with Alpha Triad gone, you're in charge of the Warriors. You can call a Review Board. All you have to do is pick two other Warriors to sit on it with you.''

Rikki sighed. "This really isn't necessary," he reiterated.

Ares gazed at the dead Tiller, his anguished eyes betraying his intense inner turmoil. He turned to Rikki. "Please, Rikki. For my own peace of mind.''

Rikki was surprised by the distress Ares was suffering. Everyone had always considered Ares to be callous, to be impervious to any emotional affliction. They were certainly wrong. "I will call a Review Board for tomorrow," he said.

"Thank you," Ares stated, relieved. "I am in your debt.''

Bertha, Spartacus, Teucer, and a score of Family members reached the scene of the tragedy and clustered around, everyone asking questions at once.

Yama took hold of Lieutenant Farrow's right hand. "We must get you to the Healers.''

Farrow reluctantly allowed herself to be led toward the drawbridge. She examined the ragged tear in her left forearm. "It's no big deal," she said.

"Who are you kidding?" Yama retorted, weaving through the gathering crowd.

"You might be needed here," Farrow said.

"Rikki will handle it," Yama declared. He grinned at her. "What's the matter? Are you afraid of seeing the Healers?''

"I'm not too fond of having needles stuck into me," Farrow acknowledged.

"Our Healers don't use needles," Yama informed her.

"What kind of medicine do they use?" Farrow asked.

"Herbal remedies, primarily," Yama answered. "They employ a varied assortment of natural medicines.''

"And they don't jab you with needles?" Farrow inquired.

"No."

"Then how do you take your medicine?" she queried.

"Orally," Yama responded. "Usually their remedies are incorporated into a tea. Otherwise, they make pills."

"And these remedies work?" Farrow asked.

"Every time," Yama said, "and without the adverse reactions people often suffered before the Big Blast to artificial chemicals and stimulants."

"Our scientists maintain herbal medicine is quackery," Farrow commented without real conviction.

"Let the Healers treat you," Yama proposed, "then you be the judge."

They reached the drawbridge and started across. More Family members were hastening to the field. Sherry, Hickok's wife, approached.

"What happened?" Sherry asked as she came abreast of Yama.

Yama nodded at Farrow's left arm. "See Rikki. We must reach the infirmary."

"I understand," Sherry said, and ran off.

"Your Family is really tight-knit," Farrow mentioned as they hastened in the direction of C Block.

"We're taught in childhood to love one another," Yama told her.

"Love? Isn't that strange talk coming from a Warrior?"

Yama shook his head. "Why should the quality of love be incompatible with being a Warrior?"

"Because your whole purpose in life is to kill," Farrow said. "You're like me. A trained fighter. Killing is all we know."

Yama paused and looked into her eyes. "If all you know is killing, I feel sorry for you."

"I don't need your sympathy!" Farrow snapped, withdrawing her hand from his.

Yama continued toward the infirmary.

"How do you do it?" Farrow asked, staying on his

heels.

"Do what?"

"Justifying killing, if you think so highly of love?" Farrow inquired.

"All of the Warriors learn to love before they learn to kill," Yama revealed. "Our early years with our parents and in the Family school are devoted to learning about love. What it is, how—"

"What is love?" Farrow interrupted.

"You don't know?" Yama rejoined.

"I'm serious. What is love? There are so many definitions," Farrow observed.

"We define love as doing good for others," Yama disclosed. "It's our golden rule. Do for others as you conceive your actions to be guided by the Spirit. Every child in the Family memorizes this teaching by the time they're seven."

"But if you're all taught so much about love," Farrow said, "how is it the Warriors become so adept at killing?"

"The Family exalts the ideal of spiritual love," Yama stated, recalling his philosophy classes under Plato's instruction. "Unfortunately, the rest of this crazy world doesn't see it our way. If the Family is to survive in an insane world where violence is supreme and hatred is rampant, then some members must be willing to do whatever is necessary to preserve our Home and our ideals. The Warriors are skilled killers, true, but we only kill because we love our Family and want to safeguard them from the degenerates out there." He waved toward the west wall.

"You kill because you love," Farrow said thoughtfully. "That's a new one." She clamped her right hand over the wound on her left arm to stem the flow of blood. The mutant had torn a six-inch gash in her forearm, and although she was still bleeding, the blood flowing down her arm and dripping from her elbow, there wasn't as much as before.

"We're almost there," Yama said, pointing at C Block.

"There's no hurry," Farrow said. "It's almost

stopped bleeding.''

"Tell me," Yama stated. "Why do you kill?"

Farrow was taken unawares by the question. "I never gave it much consideration," she admitted. "I guess I kill because I'm a professional soldier. It's what I'm trained to do."

"Do you like to kill?"

"Not particularly," she confessed. "It's my job."

"Do you love the Technics?" Yama asked.

"Love the Technics? You mean the way you do the Family?" Farrow laughed. "Not hardly! They're all so damn selfish and self-centered! There's not much to love!"

They were nearly to the infirmary doorway. Yama stopped and stared at Farrow. "So you kill because it's what they trained you to do, but you don't really like killing and you don't much like the Technics you kill for?"

Farrow did a double take. "I never looked at it that way."

"What other way is there to look at it?" Yama retorted. "Frankly, I don't see how you live with your soul."

"What do you mean?"

"Look at yourself. Take a good, hard look. You're in a rut, stuck in a vocation you care little for, serving people you like even less. Where's your sense of self-worth? Where's your dignity as a cosmic daughter of our Maker?" He shook his head. "I don't see how you do it." He stepped to the doorway. "Come on."

"Yama . . ." Farrow said tentatively.

He hesitated, standing in the doorway to the giant cement Block. "Yes?"

"Thank you."

"For what?"

"For saving my life back there," Farrow said.

"You saved mine," he reminded her.

"And . . ." she began groping for the right words, "and for opening a window."

Now it was his turn to show bewilderment. "A window?"

"Yeah. A window to the soul I never knew I had."
Farrow smiled, genuine affection lighting her dark eyes.
"Thank you," she reiterated softly, gently.

Yama's blue eyes touched hers. "Any time."

7

"How much longer before we reach Chicago?" Blade demanded, concentrating on steering the SEAL around the multiple obstacles in the highway; there were ruts and cracks, potholes and mini-trenches, and even whole sections of former U.S. Highway 12 were buckled and impassable or missing, necessitating constant detours to avoid the problem spots.

"We should reach the outskirts of Technic City soon," Captain Wargo replied.

The SEAL had been on the road for three days, three relatively uneventful days of traveling while the sun was up and pulling over to rest at night. They deliberately skirted the larger cities in their path, knowing from painful experience such urban centers were invariably dominated by violent street gangs or other hostile parties. The smaller towns and hamlets they encountered were usually devoid of life and in abject disrepair. Three towns did show signs of current habitation, but the occupants had obviously fled at the sight of the gargantuan green SEAL, its huge tires, tinted body, sophisticated solar panels, and militaristic contours all lending an ominous aspect to its appearance.

Blade was behind the steering wheel. Across from him, on the other side of a console, Captain Wargo was seated in the other bucket seat. Hickok and Geronimo occupied a wide seat behind the bucket seats. The rear of the SEAL was devoted to storage space for their supplies.

"Technic City?" Hickok spoke up. "I thought we're headin' for Chicago?"

"Chicago was renamed long ago," Captain Wargo said, "although some people still refer to it by that antiquated name."

"You didn't tell us this earlier," Blade observed.

Wargo shrugged. "I didn't think it was important."

Blade repressed a frown. The more he came to know Wargo, the less he trusted the Technic. There was a sly, devious quality about the officer. So far, despite tactful probing by the three Warriors, Captain Wargo had stuck to his original story; the Technics wanted the Family's assistance in retrieving the Genesis Seeds. Blade didn't believe him for a moment, and had given orders for one of the Warriors to always be inside the SEAL even when they were parked for the night or taking "a nature break." If Wargo intended to steal the SEAL, Blade wanted to insure the Technic never got the chance. But during their three-day journey Wargo had behaved himself.

Blade was beginning to wonder if he was wrong about the man.

"Our Minister is looking forward to seeing you," Captain Wargo commented.

"Do tell," Hickok quipped.

"He will reward you richly for your services," Wargo said.

"We'll be satisfied with our share of the Genesis Seeds," Blade commented.

"Of course," Captain Wargo said, grinning.

Blade wanted to punch the smug so-and-so right in the mouth.

"Will we be staying in Chicago . . . Technic City . . . long?" Geronimo asked.

"No," Blade responded before Wargo could speak. "I want to reach New York City as quickly as possible."

"There's no rush," Captain Wargo said pleasantly.

"There is for us," Blade rejoined. "We want to get in, grab the Seeds, and get out. It'll take us five days, maybe more, to reach New York. Another day to find the Seeds. Then five more days to Technic City and three more to the Home. All tolled, we'll be gone from our Home about three weeks. I don't like being away from the Home so long. The sooner we get back, the better."

"I can appreciate your feelings," Captain Wargo said, "but some things can't be rushed. It may take us more than one day to locate the Genesis Seeds in New York."

"You told us you know where they're located," Blade reminded him.

"We believe we know," Captain Wargo amended his statement. "We think our earlier teams did find the building they're in, but we really won't know for certain until we descend to the underground vault and examine it."

"Terrific!" Hickok muttered. "We come all this way, and it could all be a wild-goose chase!"

Captain Wargo twisted in his seat and glanced at each of them. "Don't you understand how important this is?"

Hickok chuckled. "How can we forget with you remindin' us every two seconds?"

Captain Wargo's jaw muscles tightened. "I'm sorry if I seem to dwell on the subject, but the future of mankind is at stake."

Geronimo suddenly leaned forward, pointing directly ahead. "Do you see what I see?"

Blade nodded. He'd seen it too. A giant metal fence across the highway ahead, its gleaming strands stretching into the distance on both sides of U.S. Highway 12.

"What the dickens is that?" Hickok queried.

As the SEAL drew nearer, Blade could ascertain more details. The fence was 15 feet high and tipped with four strands of barbed wire. Bright gray in color, the fence was a heavy-gauge mesh affair with peculiar metallic globes or balls imbedded in the mesh at ten yard intervals. Each of these globes was a yard in diameter.

"You'd better slow down," Captain Wargo advised. "They're expecting us, but they might not recognize the SEAL and open fire."

Blade could see a gate in the fence, and behind the gate, which was constructed of the same mesh as the fence, reared a huge guard tower. Over 30 feet in height and positioned on the left side of the road, it was manned with machine guns and several figures in uniform.

"You can stop now," Captain Wargo directed.

Blade applied the brakes, bringing the transport to a halt ten yards from the gate. "Do you have a fence blocking every road into the city?" he asked.

"We have a fence completely encircling the city," Captain Wargo answered.

"You mean this fence goes all the way around Chicago?" Hickok asked the Technic.

"Technic City is surrounded by this fence," Captain Wargo said. "It was built to keep unwanted intruders out. Do you see those regulators in the fence?"

"Those big metal balls?" Hickok stated.

"Yes. They're precision voltage regulators. Our fence is electrified with one million volts of electricity. If you were to so much as tap on the fence, you'd be fried to a crisp within seconds," Captain Wargo told them.

"One million volts?" Blade's mind was boggled by this revelation. The Family owned a functioning generator confiscated from soldiers in Thief River Falls, but fuel was scarce and they only used the generator on special occasions. Normally, they utilized candles and fires for their nightly illumination, and their plows and wagons ran on literal horsepower. The Civilized Zone produced electricity for its larger cities and towns, but their power plants were few and far between, their equipment outdated, and they suffered periodic outages on a regular basis.

"Perhaps you would like to visit one of our generating facilities?" Captain Wargo asked.

"How many do you have?" Blade inquired.

"Two. Between them, they produce more electricity than we can use. Most of it is diverted to our Atmospheric Control Stations."

"Incredible!" Blade acknowledged.

Captain Wargo reached for the door handle. "If you

don't mind, I will have the guards open the gate."

"Go ahead," Blade said.

Captain Wargo exited the SEAL and walked toward the gate.

"You reckon that varmint was tellin' the truth about one million volts in that fence?" Hickok asked.

"Why don't you touch the fence and find out?" Geronimo cracked.

Blade looked at the gunman. "I believe him," he said.

Hickok whistled. "If they can spare a million volts for a measly fence, what's it gonna be like in there?"

"We'll soon know," Blade commented, poking his head outside.

Captain Wargo approached the gate, his arms upraised until he stopped in front of it. He conversed with someone on the tower stairway, and within moments the gate was thrown open, clearing a wide path for the SEAL. Captain Wargo turned and waved, beckoning them forward.

"Stay alert," Blade cautioned his companions. He drove the SEAL to the gate and braked.

Captain Wargo climbed inside. "They've radioed the Minister. He'll be expecting us."

Hickok, studying the guard tower, suddenly gave a start and opened his mouth as if to speak. Instead, his eyes narrowed and he placed his right thumb on the hammer of his Henry, snuggled in his lap.

Blade accelerated, the transport cruising through the gate and into the unknown.

U.S. Highway 12 underwent a fantastic transformation, from a neglected roadway abused by over a century of abandonment to a perfectly preserved asphalt surface complete with white and yellow lines down the center of the highway.

Captain Wargo noticed the surprise flicker over the giant Warrior's features. "All of the roads in Technic City are maintained in excellent condition," he remarked.

Blade spotted a line of low buildings, perhaps 250 yards from the fence. Between the electrified fence and the buildings was a field of green grass, the grass interspersed with yellow, red, and blue flowers. Butter-flies flitted in the air.

Captain Wargo indicated the field. "Looks peaceful, doesn't it?"

"Yes," Blade replied. "What is it, a park of some kind?"

Captain Wargo laughed. "No. It's a mine field."

"A mine field?" Blade repeated.

"It's our secondary line of defense," Captain Wargo explained. "Should any attackers get past the fence, they'd have to cross a field dotted with thousands of mines. The field, like the fence, surrounds the city."

Blade stared at a patch of flowers, pondering. If the mine field was intended to keep enemies out, then why wasn't it located outside the electrified fence? Why place it inside, where an unwary citizen, child, or pet could stumble into it and be blown to kingdom come? The mine field's position didn't make any sense—unless it was intended to keep people *in*.

The SEAL reached the line of buildings.

"These are individual residential structures," Captain Wargo detailed.

The buildings were unlike any Blade had ever seen, including those in the Civilized Zone. While the homes in the Civilized Zone were made of brick or wood or steel, these were composed of a synthetic compound similar to the SEAL's plastic body. Each building was only one-story high, and they were characterized by a diversity of colors and shapes with circles, squares, and triangles predominating. Windows were tinted in different shades. Yards were meticulously kept up, replete with cultivated gardens and lush green grass. The setting was tranquil, ideal for family life.

Only one thing was missing.

People.

"Guards," Hickok warned.

Blade saw four soldiers ahead and slowed.

"It's just a checkpoint," Captain Wargo declared. "You can keep going."

Blade drove past the quartet of troopers, who

snapped to attention and saluted as the transport passed.

"Flashing lights coming this way," Geronimo announced. "Three of them."

Vehicles of some sort were rapidly approaching from the east.

"Don't worry," Captain Wargo assured them. "It's just our escort."

"We need an escort?" Blade asked.

"Trust me," Captain Wargo said. "You'll understand better in a couple of minutes."

The vehicles turned out to be blue cycles. Blade had seen motorcycles before, but not like these. Instead of two wheels, each blue cycle had three. Their frames sat lower to the ground than the two-wheelers, and each one was outfitted with a miniature windshield. Riders in light blue uniforms with blue helmets were on each bike, and they guided their tri-wheelers with expert skill and precision, wheeling into a tight U-turn in front of the SEAL and assuming a line across the highway. The red and blue flashing lights were affixed to the front of the tri-wheelers, directly above the single front wheel.

"They're Technic police," Captain Wargo stated. "Just follow them and they'll clear the road."

"What the blazes are they drivin'?" Hickok asked.

"Trikes," Captain Wargo responded.

"Be careful you don't squish 'em," Hickok told Blade. "Our tires are bigger than them teensy contraptions."

"There's a reason for that," Captain Wargo said.

"I'd love to hear it," Hickok mentioned.

"You'll see in a bit," Captain Wargo said.

The Technic police gunned their trikes, and Blade fell in behind them. They traveled for over a mile, passing hundreds of seemingly vacant residential structures.

"You're about to see why we need your help," Captain Wargo commented.

"How do you mean?" Blade asked.

"While our technology is superior to anyone else's," Captain Wargo bragged, "we don't possess unlimited resources. Our vehicles reflect our dilemma. Ahhh.

Here. You'll see.''

The Technic police had braked at an intersection.

Blade did likewise, scanning the area ahead, stunned by the sight before them.

Another quartet of soldiers was stationed at the intersection, two of them standing to the right, two to the left, idly watching the traffic. And traffic there was! Vehicle after vehicle. Red, brown, yellow, purple, green, black; every color in the rainbow and more. But they weren't the traditional vehicles Blade had observed elsewhere. The Warriors had appropriated a number of jeeps and trucks during the war against the Civilized Zone. Most of those had been returned after the two sides signed a peace treaty. President Toland had given two troop transports and two jeeps to Plato as a gesture of good will, but they were driven sparingly for two reasons. Plato didn't want the Family to develop a dependence on motorized transportation after more than a century without any, and, secondly, although the Civilized Zone operated a few refineries, their fuel output was minimal and barely served their own needs, restricting the scant amounts they could trade with the Family. So, while Blade was familiar with jeeps and trucks and cars, and knew traffic in large cities in the Civilized Zone was quite heavy, none of his prior experience had prepared him for *this!*

Trikes were the order of the day. Thousands upon thousands. Another vehicle, a cycle similar to a trike but with four wheels, was also in plentiful evidence. The four-wheelers had two seats, front and back, and could seat up to six occupants. The trikes and four-wheelers packed the highways. Each road appeared to handle traffic flowing in only one direction. The intersection would have been a madhouse, except for a yellow traffic light suspended above the middle of the junction, its red, yellow, and green lights apparently signaling directions to the drivers. When the traffic light facing one of the roads was red, Blade noticed, the vehicles on that road would stop. When the light was green, the trikes and four-wheelers would resume their travel.

"I don't believe it!" Geronimo said.

"Now you see what I meant," Captain Wargo stated. "We lack the resources to provide cars and trucks for our citizens, so we do the next best thing. Cycles don't require unlimited raw material, and they consume far less fuel than cars or trucks. We can manufacture enough cycles for everyone at a fraction of the cost a full-sized vehicle would demand."

"Does everyone own a cycle?" Blade asked, half in jest.

"Everyone of legal age, yes," Captain Wargo answered.

"Doesn't anybody around here know how to walk?" Hickok joked.

"Why walk when technology can provide a preferable alternative?" Captain Wargo responded. "Besides, vagrancy is illegal."

"Are you tellin' me it's against the law to walk?" Hickok inquired.

"Of course not!" Captain Wargo said, scoffing at the idea. "You can walk anywhere, anytime. Of course, you need to obtain the proper permit first."

"Of course," Hickok said.

Blade faced the Technic officer. "Why is there only traffic on the other three roads? Why are we the only ones on this one?"

"It should be obvious," Wargo said. "This road is an exit road. It leads to the fence. Why would anyone want to use this road?"

"What if they want to leave Technic City?" Blade queried.

"No one leaves the city," Captain Wargo said archly. "Why should they want to leave? You know how dangerous it is out there. We didn't have much trouble because even the wild animals and the mutants fled from the SEAL. But for someone on foot, it would be certain suicide."

"They could use a trike or four-wheeler," Blade suggested.

"Taking a vehicle outside of the city is strictly forbidden," Captain Wargo said, "unless you get a permit beforehand."

"Of course," Hickok interjected sarcastically.

For the briefest instant, a fleeting rage burned in Wargo's eyes. The look vanished as swiftly as it appeared.

The three Technic police abruptly pulled ahead, their lights flashing and their sirens sounding. All traffic ground to a halt, leaving the intersection free of vehicles. The Technic police headed due east, and it was as if a huge hand were parting a sea of cycles. The trikes and four-wheelers scooted to the sides of the highway, some to the left and some to the right, opening an aisle for the Technic police and the SEAL.

"Follow them," Captain Wargo directed.

Blade complied. He gazed at the vehicles lining the sides of the road and received a rude shock. Instead of staring at the SEAL, as any ordinary, curious person would do, the occupants of the trikes and four-wheelers averted their faces, deliberately turning away from the transport.

Or were they turning away from the police?

Blade was feeling distinctly uneasy. Something was definitely wrong here, but he couldn't put his finger on the exact cause. He doubted the Warriors were in any real danger; none of the troopers or vehicles they had seen so far could pose any threat to the SEAL. The transport's shatterproof structure could easily withstand small-arms fire. And the trikes and four-wheelers would be as fleas assaulting a grizzly if they endeavored to impede the SEAL. The Warriors were safe for the time being, but realizing the fact didn't dispel his nervousness.

The scenery shifted, the residential buildings being replaced by larger edifices, up to four stories high and covering several acres. They were either white, gray, or black.

"This is part of our manufacturing sector," Captain Wargo informed them.

Blade recalled seeing photographs in the Family library depicting prewar industry. "Where are the smokestacks?" he asked. "And how do you keep your factories so clean? I thought they were usually gritty and grimy, and made a lot of noise. Yours are so quiet."

Captain Wargo smiled. "You're comparing our modern, computerized, transistorized, and miniaturized factories to the obsolete monoliths prevalent before World War III. That's like comparing worms to shrimp. There just is no comparison," he stated with pride.

Worms to shrimp? What a strange analogy! Blade watched as the Technic police continued to part the traffic ahead. "This doesn't look like the Chicago I remember reading about when I was little," he commented.

"It isn't," Captain Wargo declared. "We rebuilt it from the ground up. The old ways were wasteful, inefficient. They deserved to be replaced." Wargo paused and looked at the passing factories. "Chicago wasn't hit during the war, but a lot of the city was damaged by the looters, the hordes of scavengers, the roving gangs, and the mutants after the war was over. When the Technics came to power, they knew they had to rebuild from scratch. Out with the old and in with the new."

"It must have taken an immense work force to accomplish all of this," Blade mentioned.

Wargo grinned and waved his right hand to the right and the left. "As you can see, our work force now numbers in the millions."

"All of these people?" Blade inquired, glancing at the ocean of humanity lining both sides of the highway.

"All of them. It's against the law for anyone not to work. Being unemployed is a major crime," Captain Wargo disclosed.

"What about your children?" Geronimo entered their conversation.

"What about them?" Wargo replied.

"Where are they?" Geronimo probed. "I didn't see any playing in the yards in the residential area. Where are they?"

"Depends on their age," Captain Wargo said. "Those over twelve hold down full-time jobs. Those under twelve are in school."

"What about the infants?" Geronimo asked.

"They're in school," Captain Wargo reiterated.

"Even those two years old?" Geronimo questioned.

"Compulsory day-care begins at six months," Captain Wargo said.

"Six months?" Geronimo exchanged astonished looks with Hickok. "How do the parents feel about that?"

"They don't have any say in the matter," Wargo replied.

"You mean the young'uns are stuck in day-care whether the parents like it or not?" Hickok demanded.

Wargo snorted. "Parents! What the hell do they know! The government knows what's best for the children, not the parents. We don't place the same emphasis on parenting your Family does."

"Do tell," Hickok retorted.

"In fact," Captain Wargo began, then hesitated, debating the wisdom of finishing his sentence. He shrugged and went on. "In fact, our children aren't raised by their natural parents."

"What?" Blade joined in.

"Biological bonding inhibits their effectiveness as productive citizens," Captain Wargo said. "The kids are brought up by appointed surrogate parents. This way, we avoid all that messy emotional garbage other societies are tainted with."

"I think they call that garbage love," Blade remarked icily.

"Don't take offense at our system," Captain Wargo stated. "Just because it's different than yours doesn't mean we can't live together in peace."

Blade's fingers tightened on the steering wheel. An intense revulsion swept over him. These Technics were worse than the government of the Civilized Zone had once been, and the Civilized Zone had been ruled by a dictator! How could they forcibly take innocent children away from their parents? How could they intentionally deprive the children of the caring and sharing during their formative years, qualities so essential to their later adult life? What kind of mon—

What in the world was *that*?!

The building was tremendous in size and magnificent in design. Ten stories in height, it reared skyward from its wide base and tapered to a point. The base was two acres in circumference, the structure progressively narrowing as it ascended. Its sides shone in the sunlight, resembling scintillating crystal. The doors lining the base were gold plated, as were the frames of all the windows. The sheer brilliance of the building dazzled the senses.

"Wow!" Hickok exclaimed.

"It's our Central Core," Captain Wargo revealed. "The seat of our government. Our Minister resides within."

"Are there any more of these?" Blade asked, dumfounded.

Captain Wargo laughed. "No. All administrative functions are handled from here."

"You say the Minister is waitin' for us in there?" Hickok inquired.

"A banquet will be held in your honor tonight," Captain Wargo answered. "We have quite a reception planned for you."

"Only two of us will be able to attend," Blade stated.

"Why can't all three of you come?" Wargo inquired politely.

"One of us must stay with the SEAL," Blade replied.

"The Minister will be very disappointed," Wargo commented.

"One of us must stay with the SEAL," Blade stressed.

Captain Wargo shrugged. "Whatever you want. But I don't see why you can't lock the doors and leave the SEAL unattended. It will be safe, I assure you."

"Thanks, but no," Blade said.

The Technic police reached a spacious parking lot surrounding the Central Core. Trikes and four-wheelers were parked in droves, and mixed among them were a few jeeps and trucks.

"What are those?" Hickok asked, leaning forward. "You said you didn't make them."

"I never said that," Captain Wargo answered. "We

don't produce them in quantity, but we do have a few. Trikes and four-wheelers can't serve all our needs.''

Blade followed the police escort into the parking lot. The area was crawling with men and women in blue uniform. Civilians filled the sidewalks, hurrying to and fro, engaged in their daily activities.

''Pull in there,'' Captain Wargo instructed, pointing at a wide expanse of parking lot devoid of trikes. It was situated in front of the middle of the Central Core, not far from a pair of gold doors. ''It's been reserved for you.''

Blade drove to the spot indicated and braked, aligning the transport so the front end faced the Central Core.

The trio of Technic police positioned their trikes around the SEAL. They were joined by dozens of others, some coming from the parking lot, others from the Central Core. Within minutes, they had formed into a blue phalanx enclosing the SEAL on four sides.

''See?'' Captain Wargo said. ''No one will bother the SEAL.''

''Not even if they get a permit first?'' Hickok quipped.

Captain Wargo's right hand surreptitiously moved to his rear pocket. He slid his fingers inside and clasped a brown plastic ball with a solitary red button. Slowly, proceeding cautiously, he removed the object and eased his hand toward the floor.

Blade turned in his seat. ''Geronimo, you stay here and keep an eye on the SEAL. Keep the doors locked. You know what to do,'' he said meaningfully.

Geronimo nodded. ''The SEAL is in good hands. Don't worry.''

Blade nodded. ''Hickok, you're with me.''

Hickok patted his Henry. ''Like a shadow.''

Captain Wargo opened his door. ''Whenever you're ready?''

''My Commando,'' Blade said to the gunman.

Hickok twisted and reached over the back of his seat into the rear section. Blade's Commando was lying on top of the pile of food, ammunition, and spare clothing.

He grabbed it by the barrel and swung it around. "Here."

Blade took the gun. "Thanks. Let's go." He threw his door open and dropped to the ground.

Hickok followed suit.

"Last chance to change your mind," Captain Wargo said to Geronimo with a friendly smile, while his right hand crept under his bucket seat.

"I must stay here," Geronimo replied.

Captain Wargo nodded. "Suit yourself. You'll miss some great food, though." He pressed the red button on the plastic ball and gently placed it on the floor under the seat. "See you later." He clambered from the transport and closed the door.

Blade and Hickok walked to the front of the SEAL, next to the grill, their weapons at the ready, and waited for the Technic officer to reach them.

"You're in for a treat," Captain Wargo announced as he led the way toward the Central Core.

Blade glanced over his left shoulder and saw Geronimo locking the doors and rolling up the widows. Good. There was no way the Technics could break into the transport with the doors and windows secure, leaving Geronimo as snug as the proverbial bug.

The Technic police, all at attention, parted, allowing Captain Wargo and the two Warriors to cross the parking lot to the sidewalk and reach the gold doors.

"Is this real gold?" Hickok asked.

"We don't believe in imitations," Wargo cryptically responded. He extended his left arm and touched one of a series of buttons in a panel to the left of the doors. Immediately, the doors hissed open. "Pneumatically controlled," he said for their benefit, and entered.

Blade paused, examining the layout. Ahead was a huge foyer or lobby, lavishly adorned, but oddly empty. Across the room was a row of cubicles with lighted numerals projecting from the wall overhead.

The gunman also noted the cubicles. "I know what they are," Hickok said. "I've seen 'em before. They're called elevators."

Captain Wargo walked across the lobby toward the

elevators.

Blade and Hickok tentatively tagged after the officer.

"We'll take an elevator up to the reception room," Wargo said. He strode to the righthand elevator and stepped inside.

Blade and Hickok, constantly surveying the lobby, staying side by side, stepped up to the elevator.

"Can't we take some stairs?" Blade asked.

"Climb ten floors?" Captain Wargo replied. He snickered. "You can, if you want to. But I'm not about to climb ten flights when there's an elevator handy."

Blade hesitated, then entered the elevator.

Hickok strolled in, studying the overhead light, the bank of lit buttons on the right side, and the small grill in the center of the floor.

Captain Wargo smiled reassuringly. "There's nothing to be nervous about. Believe me, you'll never know this ride took place." His right hand stabbed one of the buttons.

The elevator door started to close. And that's when it happened.

Captain Wargo dived, his arms outstretched. His hurtling form narrowly missed the closing door.

Blade leveled the Commando, but the gunman was faster. The Henry boomed, but the closing door intervened, the slug hitting the edge of the door and careening outside.

The elevator door slammed shut.

"Blast!" Hickok fumed. "We're trapped!"

Blade pounded on the right wall, then the door. "They're too thick to break through," he commented methodically.

Hickok stared straight up. "What about the light?"

Blade inspected the overhead light. It was rectangular, about two feet in width. A man might be able to squeeze—

There was a loud thump from underneath the elevator.

"What the blazes was that?" Hickok asked.

"I don't know," Blade said.

Another distinct thump sounded.

"I don't like this, pard," Hickok remarked.

"We walked right into this one," Blade admitted, frowning. "I think they're after the SEAL, but they'll never get it. I left the keys inside with Geronimo."

"I hope you're right," Hickok stated, bending over to peer at the buttons. "Should I push one of these?"

"Go for it."

Hickok punched the button marked OPEN.

Nothing happened.

"Uh-oh," the gunman said.

Blade, scrutinizing the overhead light, felt a slight burning sensation in his nostrils.

"A bullet would ricochet off these walls," Hickok was saying. "Say, do you smell somethin'?"

Blade glanced down.

Curling, wispy white tendrils were emanating from the grill in the elevator floor. They rose toward the ceiling, spreading, congealing into a cloudy mass.

Damn! Blade crouched and laid his hands over the small grill, striving to cover the slits with his fingers and stifle the smoke. He was only partially successful. The smoke continued to seep out, filling the elevator.

"What a lousy way to go!" Hickok said, and coughed. His eyes were watering, his nose tingling, and his lungs gasping for fresh air.

Blade was feeling dizzy. He weaved unsteadily and put his left hand over his mouth and nose.

"Do . . . you . . . think it's . . . poisonous?" Hickok asked, doubling over and collapsing on his knees.

"Don't . . . know," Blade croaked, his throat parched and raspy.

The elevator was a muggy, misty white haze.

Blade's legs buckled and he fell to the floor. He wished he could apologize to Hickok. He'd stupidly led the gunman into a trap any amateur would have avoided. There was only one consolation. The bastards would never get the SEAL. Geronimo was locked inside safe and sound.

It served the bastards right!

Blade struggled to rise, but his limbs refused to obey, and he pitched onto his face with a protracted sigh.

8

Lieutenant Alicia Farrow was in a dire quandary.

What the hell was she supposed to do?

Farrow ran her right hand through her crewcut black hair, her dark eyes troubled.

What *was* she going to do?

Farrow was seated on the bank of the inner moat, 50 yards north of the drawbridge, her back leaning against the trunk of a tall maple tree. She stared at the slowly meandering water, dejected.

Her ass was grass!

She had deliberately violated her orders! The Minister would boil her in oil when he found out! Violating an order was an offense in the first degree, punishable by death.

Her death.

Farrow closed her eyes, deep in reflection. According to her instructions, she should have given the signal yesterday. Somewhere out there, lurking in the trees, waiting for her to activate her beeper, was the four-member demolition crew. What were their names? Sergeant Darden was one. And Private Rundle was another. There was a loudmouth named Johnson, and one other whose name eluded her. They would be wondering why she didn't signal. How long before they sent someone to check on her? How long before they discovered she was derelict in her duty?

But how could she do it?

How could she give the signal, knowing the

compound would be demolished by a series of devastating explosions?

How could she give the signal, knowing what it would mean to her newfound friends?

Dammit!

Why did she have to go and become attached to these people? She'd never acted this way before! She was allowing raw emotionalism to pervert her higher purpose.

But she couldn't help herself.

There was something intangible about the Family, some elusive quality supremely attractive in its simplicity. Maybe it was the way they all cared for one another. Really cared. Not the fake bullshit so common among the Technics, but authentic affection. She'd seen it. She'd experienced it. A peculiar sensation, new to her, alien in its profound impact on her mind and heart.

Was it—she balked at mentally framing the word—was it love? Real love? Not the artificial crap she'd known all her life. But sincere, unaffected, pure love?

Whatever it was, it scared the daylights out of her!

She felt it most when in Yama's presence. Incredibly, she couldn't get enough of him. She concocted excuses to be near him. Asked him questions to draw out their conversations, when she already knew the answers. She wanted to be near him every second of every day.

What the hell had happened to her?

Farrow opened her eyes and gazed at the moat. She had a decision to make, and she couldn't afford to wait any longer. Either she sent the signal, or she told Yama about the demolition team.

One or the other.

But which?

"Mind some company?" asked a deep voice.

Farrow glanced up, and there he was, the morning sun to his rear, adding a preternatural glow to the outline of his muscular physique, his dark blue garment bulging with power, his silver hair and mustache neatly combed, freshly washed.

Farrow couldn't force her mouth to function. She

swallowed, nodding.

Yama sat down next to her, laying his Wilkinson on the grass. "I was searching all over for you. Is everything all right?"

Farrow averted her eyes. "Fine," she responded huskily.

"Are you sure?" Yama insisted.

"I'm okay," Farrow asserted. "Why do you ask?"

"Just a feeling I have," Yama said. He scrutinized her features for a moment. "Are you homesick?"

"What?" Farrow replied in surprise.

"Are you homesick? Do you miss your fellow Technics? Is that why you're upset?" Yama inquired.

"I'm not upset," Farrow rejoined stiffly.

"Whatever you say," Yama said.

Farrow nervously bit her lower lip, then glanced at him. "I don't miss them," she confided. "Truth to tell, I don't even want to go back."

"Then don't."

Farrow laughed bitterly. "Oh, yeah! Just like that!"

"Why not?" Yama asked.

"They might not like it," Farrow said.

"So what? It's your life. You can do whatever you want," Yama declared.

"That's easy for you to say," Farrow stated. She decided to change the subject. "I'd like to hear some more about you."

"Me? You already know more than anyone else," Yama remarked.

"But I don't know everything, and I want to know all about you," Farrow blatantly told him. "For instance, how is it you Warriors are all so different? I mean, you all attended the same Family school. You all had the same teachers. Yet each of you is as different from the other as night from day."

"It's no great mystery," Yama said, his left arm propped on the ground, relaxed. "No two people are alike. We're as unique and individual as snowflakes. Different tastes, different likes and dislikes, different interests and talents. Some people have a talent for the soil and they become Tillers. Others are tuned to psychic circuits and become Empaths. A few, like Joshua, attain harmony with the cosmos and become spiritual sages, dispensing truth to troubled souls. Then there are the Warriors. Our talent lies in the skillful manipulation of violence. Not much of a talent, when you compare it to the others. But it serves to safeguard our Home and our Family.'' He paused, staring at the west wall. ''Even similar talents can be diverse in their expression. Take the Warriors as an example. We might be termed masters of death, but each of us has perfected the mastery of a different technique in the execution of our duties, all consistent with our talents and personal preferences. Hickok is a revolver specialist. Rikki is unbeatable with a katana. Blade has his Bowies. Teucer his bow. True, we were all raised in the same environment and instructed by the same Elders, but the environment and the instructions affected us differently because we are individuals. Each of us has formed our own philosophy of life. We live according to our highest concepts of truth, beauty, and goodness. We answer to the Spirit and ourselves and no one else.'' He stopped, bemused. ''Why is it, whenever I'm near you, I can't seem to stop talking?''

''Don't stop on my account,'' Farrow said.

''I've never had this happen,'' Yama commented.

''I don't mind if you don't,'' Farrow stated, grinning.

Yama stared into her eyes. ''I'll be honest with you, Alicia. I've come to care for you a great deal. I don't want you to leave. Not just yet anyway. I'd like to get to know you better.''

Alicia turned her face away.

''I'm sorry,'' Yama said. ''I didn't mean to upset you.''

''You don't understand,'' Farrow said huskily, refusing to let him see the torment twisting her features.

''Explain it to me,'' Yama said.

''I can't.''

''Why not?'' Yama pressed her.

''Please. Leave it alone,'' Farrow pleaded. She heard his clothes rustle as he rose.

''Whatever you want,'' Yama declared. ''But I'm

always ready to listen when you decide you can trust me." His footsteps receded to the southwest.

Farrow glanced over her right shoulder, her eyes misty.

Curse her stupidity!

Now she'd done it! Gone and driven him off! Maybe antagonized him!

There was no other choice! She *must* tell him about the Minister and the demolition crew! But how would he react? Despise her for being a part of the dastardly plot? Could she risk it?

Lieutenant Alicia Farrow drew her knees up to her chest and encircled her legs with her arms. She buried her face in the stiff fabric of her fatigue pants and silently weeped, torn to the core of her being.

To give the signal, and lose her new friends and probably Yama too, or to continue wavering and face execution?

To do her duty, or as her heart dictated?

That was the question.

But what the hell was the answer?

9

He became conscious of a dull ache in the back of his head, a palpable pounding at the base of his skull. There was a bitter taste in his mouth, lingering on his tongue and lips. For a minute, he was disoriented, striving to recall where he was and what had happened.

Suddenly, he remembered in a rush.

Blade's eyes snapped open and he tried to stand, mistakenly assuming he was still on the elevator floor.

But he was wrong.

The giant Warrior had been stripped naked. He was securely locked in steel manacles, one on each wrist and around each ankle, and was suspended several inches above a white, tiled floor, his limbs spreadeagled, on a smooth blue wall.

What the . . . !????

Blade found himself a prisoner in a rectangular room. Except for a brown easy chair eight feet away, the chamber was barren of furniture. The ceiling radiated a pale, pinkish light. From somewhere off in the distance came a muted rumbling.

Where was he?

Someone groaned to his left.

Blade turned his head in the direction of the sound and found Hickok four feet away, likewise manacled to the wall.

The gunman's eyelids fluttered, then slowly opened. "Oh! My achin' noggin! Did you get a description of the buffalo that hit me?"

"Afraid not," Blade replied, chuckling.

Hickok glanced downward. "What the blazes is this?" he exploded. "I'm in my birthday suit!"

"Join the club," Blade said.

Hickok's face became a vivid scarlet. He looked up, glaring around the room. "Some bozo is gonna pay for this!"

"We really walked into this one," Blade commented regretfully.

"Don't blame yourself, pard," Hickok stated. "These sleazy turkeys set us up real good. There was nothing else you could have done."

"I don't know—" Blade began, then paused as a door on the far side of the chamber opened.

In walked four people, three men and a woman.

Blade recognized only one of them, the bastard Wargo. He was bringing up the rear of the little group, possibly indicating an inferior social status. The leader was a scarecrow of a man with a peculiar magnetic quality about him. He wore light blue pants and a blue shirt, both trimmed in gold fabric, the shirt along the end of the sleeves and the pants along the hem at the bottom. Fastened to the lapels of his shirt were gold insignia: a large *T* enclosed in a ring of gold and slashed through the center by a lightning bolt. His hair and eyes were a striking black, his hair cropped close to his head and slicked with an oily substance. A regal, leonine expression lent a lofty aspect to his appearance, but his eyes dominated his countenance. With their large, unfathomable pupils, veritable pools of black, they gazed at their surroundings with an imperious, haughty air. Their owner crossed to the easy chair and sat down. He gazed at the two Warriors and smiled. "They don't seem so formidable without their apparel," he remarked in a gravely voice.

The three others laughed.

Hickok bristled. "Let me down from here, you cow chip, and I'll show you how formidable we are!"

The man in the easy chair locked a baleful stare on the gunman.

Captain Wargo walked around the chair and up to

Hickok. Without any warning, he slugged the gun-fighter in the abdomen.

Hickok gasped and tried to double over.

"You will address the Minister with respect," Captain Wargo instructed the gunman.

Hickok, resisting an impulse to gag, looked at the Technic captain. "Go slurp horse piss, you son of a bitch!"

Wargo drew back his right fist.

"That's enough!" the Minister ordered.

Captain Wargo stiffened, wheeled, bowed to the Minister, and took up a position behind the easy chair.

Blade studied the other two. The man wore a brown outfit similar to the Minister's blue one, but without the gold trim and the insignia. He was shorter, about five feet in height, and slightly hefty. His hair was gray, his eyes blue, his cheeks full and ruddy. He stood to the right of the easy chair.

On the left side was the woman, and a lovely woman she was. Dressed in a dainty yellow blouse and a short, short green skirt, she obviously intended to accent her ample physique. Her eyes were an alert green, her hip-length hair white with a black streak down the middle.

How did she fit into the scheme of things?

"As Captain Wargo has revealed," the man in the chair said, "I am the Minister."

"Should we kiss your feet now or later?" Hickok asked.

Captain Wargo started forward, but the Minister held up his right hand, halting the officer in his tracks.

The Minister frowned. "I had hoped we could conduct this on an intelligent basis."

"That's a mite hard to do when you're sittin' on your intelligence," Hickok cracked.

The Minister glanced at Blade. "Are you going to let this buffoon do all the talking?"

"Hickok's a grown man," Blade responded. "He can say whatever he likes."

The Minister grimaced distastefully. "That's democracy for you," he said.

The three others, as if on cue, laughed.

The Minister cleared his throat. "I placed you in this position to demonstrate my complete power over you. I could have you destroyed with a snap of my fingers."

"Then why don't you?" Hickok interrupted. "Anything would be better than hangin' up here with my dingus flappin' in the air."

"Your . . . dingus . . . is the least of my concerns," the Minister said acidly. "This is an object lesson, nothing more."

"Are we supposed to be impressed?" Hickok retorted.

The Minister ignored the gunman and turned to the head of the Warriors. "You agree I could have you killed on a moment's notice?"

Blade didn't reply.

"I'll construe your silence as agreement," the Minister said. "I trust I've made my point."

"What point?" Hickok rejoined. "That you're a pervert who gets his kicks ogling folks in the nude?"

The Minister turned to Captain Wargo. "Silence this moron!"

Captain Wargo nodded and walked to the center of the left-hand wall. He touched a circular indentation and a recessed panel opened. A metallic tray emerged from the wall bearing a syringe and a box of cotton balls. The syringe was tipped with a red plastic cap.

"Why is it some varmint is always tryin' to stick me with needles?" Hickok quipped, referring to an incident during their last run.

"You leave me no recourse," the Minister declared, smirking. "Nothing personal, you understand?"

'You've got it all wrong, jackass," Hickok said harshly. "I'm takin' this humiliation real personal-like. And you'll see just how personal when you let me down from here."

"I'm trembling in abject fear!" the Minister joked.

His chorus laughed.

Captain Wargo had removed the red cap from the syringe. He walked over to the gunman and raised the syringe near his left arm.

Hickok's blue eyes narrowed. "The first thing I'm

gonna do if you let me go," he promised the Minister, "is kill you."

"Shut the fool up!" the Minister barked.

Captain Wargo plunged the syringe into the gunman's left arm, brutally, relishing the discomfort he caused.

Hickok winced, then glanced at Blade. "I'll be right here if you need me." He was about to say more, but the shot took immediate effect. His eyes drooped, then closed.

"Now that the imbecile is silenced," the Minister said, "perhaps we can proceed with a modicum of decorum?" He saw Blade examining the gunman with concern. "Don't worry about your friend. The tranquilizer Wargo administered will render Hickok unconscious for six to ten hours. He'll awaken refreshed and as obnoxious as ever."

Blade sighed in relief. He nodded at the shackle on his right wrist. "Why go to all this trouble? We were cooperating with you. We gave our word we would help find the Genesis Seeds. Why did you turn against us?"

The Minister hesitated. "Insurance," he answered at last.

"Insurance?"

"Of course. A man in my position, with so many relying on my every judgment, cannot afford to make mistakes. My people expect me to perform flawlessly, and I will not disappoint them." The Minister paused. "I know you promised to assist in retrieving the Genesis Seeds. But what's to stop you from confiscating the Seeds for yourselves after they're located?"

Blade leaned forward. "We gave you our *word*!"

"So you did. But your word means nothing to me. Actions, Blade—may I call you Blade?—speak louder than words. And there was nothing to preclude your taking action against us. I require insurance. I needed to compel your total cooperation. And I've achieved my goal."

"No you haven't," Blade said. "You can stuff your Seeds where the sun doesn't shine! We'll never cooperate now!"

The Minister smiled, displaying two rows of small, even teeth. He rolled up his left sleeve and stared at a watch. "I think you will."

"Why should we?" Blade countered. "You may have us, but Geronimo is still free. You'll never be able to stop him from leaving, from breaking through your fence and returning to the Home. The Freedom Federation will learn about your treachery. They'll put you out of business, Minister. You and this technological prison you call a city!"

The Minister grinned and shook his head. "My dear Blade! You are suffering from several delusions! First, Geronimo will not warn the Freedom Federation because he won't be leaving Technic City. Secondly, your bitterness is understandable but unwarranted. I don't intend to harm any of you. I could have done that while you were unconscious. As I already told you, this is merely a demonstration of my power. To show you what I could do if I wanted."

"What do you mean?" Blade demanded. "Why won't Geronimo be leaving Technic City?"

"You'll see shortly," the Minister stated. "Once you realize the futility of opposing me, you will assent to my wishes."

"Don't hold your breath!" Blade cracked.

The door on the other side of the room swung open, and in came three men. Two soldiers in green fatigues with a captive draped between them, sagging in their arms.

It was Geronimo.

Blade gawked at his friend, startled. "How—?"

"How did we do it?" the Minister finished the question. "Why, it was simplicity itself. Captain Wargo dropped a gas grenade in the SEAL before exiting. It was timed to release its knockout gas thirty minutes after being activated. Your poor Geronimo never knew what hit him."

Blade could readily envision the result A cloud of noxious gas filling the confines of the SEAL and over-coming Geronimo within seconds. "But the SEAL . . ."

"Ahhhh. Your vaunted vehicle!" The Minister cackled. "Presumably impenetrable."

"How did you break in?" Blade asked.

"We utilized a clothes hanger," the Minister replied.

"A what?"

"A clothes hanger. You know. Wires you hang clothes on," the Minister said gleefully.

"That's impossible!" Blade said.

"And an industrial diamond drill," the Minister added. "You see, we knew it would be useless to attempt any other method. We've heard stories about your vehicle. Bulletproof. Fireproof. But not clothes-hanger proof, eh?" He laughed uproariously, joined by his subservient trio.

Blade's mind was racing. They'd broken into the SEAL! No one had ever been able to do that! With the SEAL in enemy hands, the Warriors had lost their primary advantage. They were at the Minister's mercy!

"We drilled through the driver's window," the Minister was explaining, gloating, savoring his triumph. "I don't think you realize it, but you were unconscious six hours. In six hours an industrial diamond drill can penetrate any substance known to man, including the SEAL's unique plastic structure. Captain Wargo advised our driller on where to align his bit, and we drilled in adjacent to the door lock. Don't worry! The hole is a small one, not even noticeable unless you know where to look for it. Once the hole was drilled, we slid a straightened hanger through and unlatched the lock. An easy procedure, really. Prior to World War III, car thieves did it all the time." He chuckled. "The SEAL is now ours."

Blade, in a surge of frustration, strained against the manacles binding him. He'd failed! Failed the Family. Failed Plato. And, worst of all, failed Hickok and Geronimo. Why had he assumed the SEAL was invulnerable? He'd left it outside like a sitting duck! He'd acted like a grade-A chump! And look at what had happened!

"If you could only see the comical look on your face!" the Minister said, smiling broadly.

Fire flamed in Blade's gray eyes, and his powerful fists clenched and unclenched.

One of the troopers carrying Geronimo released his grip and marched to the easy chair. He saluted and held up a set of keys in his left hand.

The keys to the SEAL.

The Minister took the keys and waved the soldier away from his chair. "Do you see these?" He dangled the keys in the air. "I could get in the SEAL and drive it wherever I want. But I won't. Wouldn't you like to know the reason?"

"You'll tell me whether I want to know it or not."

"Be nice," the Minister cautioned. "I won't drive the SEAL off because I'm going to give the keys back to you."

"Why are you being so generous?" Blade asked sarcastically.

"Because I've proven my point. I have no need for your vehicle. You will resume your journey to New York City and retrieve the Genesis Seeds as originally planned." He paused, smirking. "Wouldn't you like to know the reason?"

Blade felt an intense rage welling within him. Had his arms been free, he would have throttled the Minister's neck. "Why?"

"Because that one," and the Minister pointed at Hickok, "will remain here. I told you I needed insurance. Well, the fool is my insurance. He will stay with us until you return. If you betray us, you will never see your friend again."

"Our relationship will be based on trust then," Blade commented dryly.

"Trust must be earned," the Minister said. "You must prove you are trustworthy, just as I have proven my reliability to you."

"You have?" Blade said skeptically.

"Certainly. I could have slain you, but didn't. I could have taken your vehicle, but I haven't. What more could I do to convince you I'm sincere?"

Blade almost laughed aloud. Sincere? The Minister was as sincere as the legendary serpent in the Garden of

Eden!

"Release him," the Minister said to Captain Wargo. "Take him next door and dress him. Then take Blade and Geronimo to the cafeteria and feed them. Have your squad report to you there. I will join you in an hour."

"As you command," Wargo said. His heels clicked together, and he moved to his left around the chair.

Blade tensed. He debated the wisdom of making a break for it, but discarded the idea. Hickok and Geronimo were both unconscious. He would be unable to carry them both to safety. Besides, there was little he could do while unarmed and naked. He would have to bide his time.

Captain Wargo produced a key and quickly unlocked the manacles securing Blade. "No hard feelings?" he asked.

Blade wanted to drive his fist into Wargo's smug face. Instead, he smiled. "No hard feelings," he lied.

"This way," Captain Wargo said, motioning for Blade to follow him.

The Minister nodded at them as they passed. He waited until Wargo, Blade, the two troopers and Geronimo were gone before he spoke again. "What did you think?" he inquired of the man in brown.

"An excellent performance," the man responded. "Blade appeared to be thoroughly confounded. He'll never suspect your true motives."

The woman raised her right hand and patted her hair into place. "I don't get it," she said in a squeaky voice.

The Minister faced her. "What don't you get?"

"Any of this," the woman said. "Why'd you hand the keys over to him? I thought you want the SEAL?"

The Minister sighed. He stood and moved next to the woman. "My one weakness," he said softly, gently placing his right hand under her chin, "and she has to be mentally deficient."

"Are you talking about me?" the woman asked in an annoyed tone.

The Minister smiled sweetly. "No, Loretta, darling," he said in a reserved manner, then abruptly thundered,

"I'm talking about the tooth fairy!"

The woman recoiled, but his hand gripped her chin, restraining her in place.

"How many times must I explain it to you?" the Minister angrily demanded.

Loretta wanted to speak, but her mouth was immobile, forced shut by the pressure on her chin.

"We have the capability of constructing a hundred SEALs," the Minister said, as if he were a teacher instructing a wayward pupil, his bearing condescending, his fingers digging into her skin. "With one exception. The SEAL is composed of a special plastic, an alloy unlike any other in existence, developed by Kurt Carpenter's scientists shortly before World War III. There isn't another vehicle like the SEAL on the face of the earth." He paused, his gaze hardening. "I want the secret of that alloy. I want to know how they made the SEAL's body. I want to duplicate their process, discover the formula they used. Once I have it in my hands, we will produce hundreds of war machines with the same plastic. We'll be unstoppable! The Freedom Federation will crumble before our armored might! And the Soviets will be next!" A fanatical gleam infested the Minister's black eyes. "We will assume our rightful place in the world! The Technics will subjugate the globe and establish a new world order! We will achieve a new and higher destiny!" He released his hold on Loretta's chin, lost in an inner rapture.

"So why don't you just take their SEAL and be done with it?" Loretta stupidly inquired.

The Minister's right hand swept up, ready to strike.

Loretta flinched, raising her right arm to protect her face. To her surprise, he lowered his hand and stepped back.

"Will you elaborate for this . . . this . . . *person*, Arthur," the Minister asked, stalking toward the door.

Arthur nodded. "We can't merely appropriate their vehicle because it might have a self-destruct mechanism."

Loretta's brow furrowed in confusion.

"The Warriors might have a way of blowing up the

SEAL if anyone attempts to steal it or drive it off,'' Arthur detailed. "Even drilling into the window entailed a calculated risk. But it also accomplished another purpose.''

"What's that?" Loretta queried.

"Even as we speak," Arthur said, "our chemists are analyzing the fragments we drilled from the window. With any luck, they'll discover the secret of the SEAL's adamantine plastic before Blade and the others return from New York City. If not . . ." He shrugged. "We will confiscate the SEAL.''

Loretta grinned. "I get it! This way, you kill two birds with one stone! The Warriors will get the canisters you need, and you'll get the chemical formula you want. With the canisters and the formula, our army will be invincible!''

"Exactly," Arthur said.

"Are you two coming?" the Minister demanded. He was standing in the doorway, holding the door open.

Loretta strolled toward him. "I'm impressed. How do you keep coming up with such brilliant plans?"

The Minister grinned. "All it requires is an exceptional intellect.''

"Do you really think they can get the canisters?" Loretta inquired.

"They'll have an excellent chance using the SEAL," the Minister said. "Once we have the canisters, we can commence work on the projectiles. Our foes will be putty in our hands.''

"It's too bad you have to go to so much trouble," Loretta remarked. "Too bad you can't just take the SEAL and be done with it.''

"True," the Minister agreed. "But we can't risk losing the SEAL before our scientists have unraveled its secrets. Captain Wargo didn't detect any evidence of any such device, but he couldn't be sure. And all Blade would have to do is press a secret button while climbing from the SEAL, and it might explode if we tampered with it.''

"So all that stuff you told Blade was to throw him off the track?" Loretta said.

"Of course."

Loretta kissed the Minister on his right cheek. "I get all tingly when I think of how lucky I am to be your consort."

"Tingly? Really?" The Minister glanced at Arthur. "Tell Wargo I will join him in two hours instead of one."

"As you command."

10

Two more days had elapsed.

Two whole days! It was the morning of the third day!
And she hadn't done a damn thing!

Lieutenant Farrow was up early. She'd spent another
sleepless night, tossing and turning on her cot in B
Block. She rose before dawn, dressed in her uniform,
and slipped from the building unnoticed. Listless,
haunted by her dereliction of duty, she strolled to the
north and eventually reached the inner moat. Standing
on the bank, she idly watched the water flowing past
and contemplated her fate. In all her years as a professional soldier, she'd never exhibited any degree of
indecision. She'd always performed her duty as required.

Until now.

Starlings were chattering in a nearby pine tree.

Farrow gazed up at the northern rampart and spotted
one of the Warriors on guard duty. It wasn't Yama; he
was still sleeping in B Block. After a moment she
recognized the figure—the lean physique, brown shirt,
buckskin pants, and broadsword dangling from his
hip—as that of Spartacus, the head of Gamma Triad.

Spartacus, his right hand resting on the hilt of his
sword, saw her and waved.

Farrow returned the gesture. Why? she wondered.
Why did these people have to be so friendly? Her job
would have been much easier if they hadn't welcomed
her with open arms. She suspected Plato and the one

called Rikki were leery of her, but the rest of the Family treated her as one of their own.

The dummies!

Didn't they know it wasn't smart to trust strangers? To trust anyone, for that matter.

Farrow sighed and sat down on the bank. She thought of the moonlit stroll she'd taken with Yama the night before, and smiled. His affection for her was becoming more obvious every day. He'd escorted her to an open-air concert between the Blocks, an evening of musical entertainment presented by six Family members with outstanding talent. The Family owned eighteen instruments in all, from drums to a miniature grand piano, and they took great pains to maintain the instruments. The Family's best Musicians were an accomplished lot, and the six had played a diverse selection of masterful compositions, their own compositions. Seated under the twinkling stars, with Yama by her side, she had been in seventh heaven.

Despite her apprehensions, Yama hadn't pried into her unstable emotional state. He seemed to be waiting for her to make the first move, to tell him what was bothering her.

And she wanted to do it.

More than anything.

But each time she opened her mouth to reveal her part in the plot against the Family, she balked, concerned she would infuriate him and kill their budding romance.

The sky was much brighter, the sun beginning to clear the eastern horizon as the world awoke to a new day.

Farrow stood and hurried toward B Block. She'd finally made up her mind. She was going to ask Yama to join her for breakfast, then spill the beans. Tell him everything. And hang the consequences! She couldn't take another night of stifling anxiety.

The Family was coming to life. Over a dozen members were clustered near B Block, some exercising, some praying, others conversing.

Farrow hurried toward B Block, afraid she would chicken out before she found Yama. Not this time! she told herself. This time she would see it through.

A flash of dark blue to her right caught her attention.

Yama was 40 yards from B Block, talking to a young woman.

Farrow stopped, frowning.

Who the hell was she?

The woman was a brunette, petite, wearing green pants and a yellow blouse. She was laughing, her right hand resting on Yama's left forearm.

What were they talking about?

Farrow slowly advanced toward them. Yama had his back to her, and the brunette was concentrating on the Warrior, so neither would detect her approach if she was careful.

She *had* to know what they were talking about.

Farrow sidled to within 15 feet of the duo, staying to the rear of Yama, using his huge body to shield her from the brunette's line of vision.

"—delighted," Yama was saying.

The brunette squealed and clapped her hands together. "You will? Honest?"

"I said I would," Yama stated.

The brunette giggled and flung her arms around the Warrior's neck. "I can never thank you enough!"

Yama's reply was too low for Farrow to overhear.

The brunette giggled some more. "You've made me so happy!"

"I'd do anything for you. You know that," Yama said.

The brunette's expression became markedly serious. "You're my favorite. You always have been."

"I'll bet you say that to all the men," Yama commented.

"You know I don't," the brunette responded playfully. "The others can't hold a candle to you."

"You may change your mind when you mature," Yama said.

"Mature?" The brunette scowled in feigned annoyance. "In case you haven't noticed, I've matured quite nicely, thank you."

"You have filled out," Yama admitted.

Farrow edged a little closer. Her mind was in a daze.

What was this? Was the little bitch making time with Yama? Did Yama have another girlfriend, one he'd neglected to mention? Was he playing the field? Was that it?

"I've always loved you," the brunette said sincerely.

"And I've always loved you," Yama told her.

Farrow felt a lump forming in her throat as the brunette stretched on her toes and planted a kiss on Yama's lips. Her mouth dropped open in shock as her darkest forebodings flooded her mind.

That had to be it!

Yama had another woman!

Farrow started to back away before she was discovered.

Yama kissed the brunette on the forehead.

He loved her! He'd always loved her! The words seemed to reverberate in Farrow's brain. There was a sharp ache in her chest. She whirled and ran to the north, toward the moat. What else could it be? They must be lovers! Yama had been leading her on!

Farrow reached a solitary maple tree and leaned on the rough trunk for support, feeling dizzy. How could she have been so gullible? She'd fallen for the oldest ruse in the book! Yama was just like every other man! They all were after one thing, and they'd get it any way they could.

By hook or by crook.

She started forward, then hesitated. What if she were wrong? There might be a perfectly innocent explanation. She twisted, glancing over her left shoulder.

Yama and the brunette were hugging.

No!

No! No! No!

Farrow stumbled toward the moat, racked by despair. How could she give him the benefit of the doubt? What more proof did she need? She'd been played for a sucker. A dupe. A patsy. For all his idealistic talk, Yama wasn't any better than a typical Technic.

He'd used her!

And nobody, but nobody, used Alicia Farrow.

She reached the moat and halted, struggling to suppress her welling anguish. No way! She wasn't about to be weak a second time! Falling for Yama's line was bad enough. She wasn't about to cry over her gullibility.

She'd get even instead!

Farrow reached into her left rear pocket and extracted a small plastic object, square in shape, two inches by two inches, a powerful transistorized transmitter with a ten-mile signal radius. Without thinking of the consequences, motivated by her burning jealousy and shattering disappointment, she depressed a black button in the middle of the transmitter.

There!

It was done!

The demolition team, if they were constantly monitoring her frequency as ordered, had received her signal. They would await the cover of darkness, then enter the compound and set their charges. By tomorrow morning, the Home would be a pile of rubble and the majority of the Family would be dead.

It served them right!

Farrow crammed the transmitter into her rear pocket, then scanned the vicinity to see if she'd been observed. No one else was nearby, but she detected a motion out of the corner of her left eye. She swung around.

Spartacus was patrolling the rampart, headed from west to east. He was 20 yards from her, his posture loose, at ease.

Apparently, he hadn't seen her activate the transmitter.

Farrow forced a grin and waved at the Warrior.

Spartacus returned her wave, his blue eyes sweeping past the Technic officer to the compound beyond. He saw the Family members gathering in the area between the Blocks for their morning socializing. There was Plato and his wife Nadine, talking with Rikki. Ares was near A Block, working out with his shortsword. And there was Yama with his niece, Marian. She was the eldest daughter of Yama's older brother. Marian was walking with Yama toward B Block, their arms linked, beaming with joy.

Spartacus grinned. He could deduce the cause for her happiness. He knew she'd been after Yama to sponsor her boyfriend for Warrior status when another opening developed. Yama had wavered, and he'd confided to Spartacus he wasn't positive the boyfriend was Warrior material. Evidently, he'd changed his mind.

Marian suddenly released Yama and dashed toward her boyfriend, who was just emerging from B Block.

Spartacus nodded with satisfaction at the accuracy of his deduction. He glanced down and saw the Technic, Farrow, staring at Yama with a pained expression on her face.

Now what was that all about?

Spartacus shrugged. It was none of his business. He'd heard the rumor going around, linking Yama and Farrow. Perhaps they were having a lover's spat. If so, he definitely wasn't about to stick his big nose into it. He was a Warrior, not a Counselor.

Besides, Yama kept that scimitar of his *real* sharp.

11

"Why are you slowing down?" Captain Wargo demanded.

"I'm going to wait until they leave the roadway," Blade replied.

"No, you're not," Captain Wargo snapped. "You're going to drive right through them."

Blade's hands tightened on the steering wheel. They were three days out of Technic City, bearing east toward New York City. So far, the going had been frustratingly slow. Most of the major highways were in deplorable condition, ruined as much by the war as 100 years of neglect and abandonment. Lengthy sections, miles at a stretch, had buckled or collapsed or were in scattered bits and pieces, necessitating countless detours. In addition to the wrecked roads, they'd encountered a surprising number of inhabited outposts, some large towns. Wargo knew where each was located; they were marked on a map he carried, along with the approximate boundary of the corridor the Soviets controlled to the south. Wargo insured Blade stayed well north of the area under Soviet domination. But the innumerable detours, to bypass the demolished roads and avoid all occupied settlements as well as the Soviets, markedly delayed their progress. They had traveled for 12 hours both days, averaging approximately 45 miles an hour. Now, by Blade's reckoning, they were within 20 miles of New York City, to the northwest of the metropolis.

Or what was left of it.

Wargo was seated in the other front bucket seat. Behind Blade and Wargo sat Geronimo and two Technic troopers, Geronimo sandwiched between them to prevent him from causing trouble. And reclining on top of the pile of supplies in the rear third of the transport was a fourth soldier, his automatic rifle in his arms.

"Well, what the hell are you waiting for?" Wargo said. "Mow them down!"

Blade surveyed the road ahead.

About 70 yards from the SEAL, walking down the middle of the highway, were two dozen men and women. They were armed with rifles and handguns, none of which posed a threat to the SEAL. Their attire was scarcely more than crudely stitched rags.

It was obvious what they were.

Scavengers.

Looters.

A motley mob preying on anyone and anything. Such marauding bands were the scourge of the post-war age, raiding established settlements and robbing and killing hapless wayfarers, like a scourge of destructive locusts.

Blade paused, not out of any sympathy for the scavengers, but because he disliked taking lives without ample justification. If the scavengers were assaulting the Home, he'd mow them down without another thought. But this was different. This would amount to nothing more than cold-blooded murder.

"Do it!" Captain Wargo barked.

Blade was about to tramp on the accelerator when the issue was resolved for him.

A mutant abruptly appeared from the trees lining the right side of the road and plowed into the scavengers.

Blade applied the brakes.

Two forms of genetic deviations had resulted from World War III. One form, designated as mutants by the Family, was the product of genetic dysfunction and aberration caused by excessive amounts of radiation unleashed on the environment. Mutants were deformed progeny of normal parents, whether human or animal. The second form, on the other hand, was the result of chemical warfare compounds distrupting ordinary organic growth, creating the creatures the Family called the mutates. Mutates were former mammals, reptiles, or amphibians transformed into ravenous, pus-covered horrors by the synthetic toxins infesting their systems.

As Blade watched what might have once been a feral dog, but was now a slavering mutate, pounce on a female scavenger and tear her neck apart with a savage wrench of its yellow fangs, he thought of one more form of genetic deviation. The type intentionally developed by the scientists, the genetic engineers, in their quest to manufacture superior life forms. Gene-splicing had been quite common before the Big Blast, and the nefarious Doktor, the Family's one-time nemesis, had refined the technique into a precision procedure, breeding a personal army of deviate assassins.

But that was then, and this was now.

The mutated canine had dispatched four of the scavengers, and the rest had fled into the trees on the left side of the road without firing a shot. The mutate pursued them.

The road ahead was clear, except for the bloody bodies.

"Get going," Captain Wargo ordered.

Blade drove forward, weaving the transport around the forms on the highway. He saw one of them as he passed, an elderly bald man whose throat was ruptured, his blood pulsing onto the highway, his lifeless brown eyes open and gaping skyward.

"I suppose now is a bad time to mention I need to wee-wee?" Geronimo asked, grinning impishly.

Captain Wargo turned in his seat. "Are you serious?"

"When Mother Nature calls," Geronimo said, "there's not much you can do about it."

"Well, it's too bad, but you'll have to hold it for a while," Wargo told him. "We're not stopping just because you need to take a leak."

"I hope I can hold it," Geronimo said. "If not, then I hope these two clowns next to me don't mind yellow stains on their uniforms."

"Just for that," Captain Wargo retorted, "you can hold it until doomsday."

"I thought that was the date of World War III," Geronimo remarked.

Wargo turned toward Blade. "Sometimes I wonder if we would have been better off leaving Geronimo behind and bringing Hickok."

"They're two of a kind," Blade mentioned.

"A kind I can do without," Wargo said. He pointed at the windshield. "Watch out for more of those scum."

"Where exactly are we?" Blade inquired, steering the SEAL around a gaping hole in the highway.

"Almost to our destination," Captain Wargo revealed. "And it didn't take us the five days you estimated it would." He smiled. "The Minister will be pleased. We'll make it back to Technic City in record time."

"If we make it back," Geronimo interjected.

"You still haven't told us where we are," Blade declared.

"That last big town we bypassed was once known as Newburgh," Captain Wargo disclosed.

"Do we take this road all the way into the city?" Blade asked.

"No." Wargo shook his head for emphasis. "The previous squads we sent in ran into a ton of trouble by using the roads. The lousy Zombies are all over the place. No. We'll play it safe and use a new approach."

"What approach?" Blade wanted to learn.

"The Hudson River," Captain Wargo said.

"The Hudson River?" Blade repeated in surprise.

"Yes," Captain Wargo affirmed. "Why do you look so shocked? We know the SEAL possesses amphibious capability. By taking the Hudson south into the heart of New York City, we reduce the number of Zombies we'll have to face. Pretty clever, I think."

"Except for one small detail," Blade said.

"Oh? What's that?"

"We've never operated the SEAL in its amphibious mode," Blade told the Technic.

Wargo snickered in disbelief. "Yeah. Sure."

Blade stared at the officer.

Captain Wargo did a double take, examining Blade's features. "You're serious, aren't you?"

"Would I lie to you?" Blade stated in mock earnestness.

"You've never operated the SEAL in the amphibious mode!" Captain Wargo reiterated, upset by the news.

"Is there an echo in here?" Geronimo queried.

Captain Wargo unexpectedly pounded the dashboard in anger. "Damn it all! We've come so close! We're almost to our goal!" He glared at Blade. "Do you realize how much trouble we went to, how much time and manpower was expended to reach this point? Getting you and this vehicle to Technic City? Managing to reach this far? Did you know the Soviet line was only five miles south of us? Sometimes we were less than a mile from their northern perimeter. And we made it past the towns and the mutants and everything else!" His voice started to rise. "I don't care if you've never operated in the amphibious mode before! Because we are not, I repeat, *not* going to give up now! Not when we're so damn close! We will adhere to the Minister's schedule."

"Your plan sounds okay to me," Geronimo interjected.

Wargo glanced at the Warrior skeptically. "It does?"

"Sure." Geronimo smirked. "*I* can swim."

Captain Wargo made a hissing sound. He faced forward, then suddenly stabbed his right index finger straight ahead. "There! That's it!"

"What?" Blade asked.

"There! Turn left there!" Wargo cried.

"Where?" All Blade saw was a crumpled roadway, dense foliage to the right, and an embankment to the left.

"There! Damn it! Turn left *now*!" Wargo shouted.

Blade complied, wrenching on the steering wheel, sending the SEAL to the left, up and over the embankment, hurtling down a steep slope toward a . . . river! He slammed on the brakes and the transport lurched to a skidding stop on the grass-covered bank.

"I must be dreaming," Geronimo said in an awed tone.

Blade gazed at the vista beyond in sheer astonishment. It wasn't the bank or the blue river causing his stupefication; it was the eerie panorama on both sides of the river to the south.

"That's the Hudson River," Captain Wargo stated.

"And what is that?" Blade asked, indicating the wrecked landscape stretching to the far southern horizon.

"That," Captain Wargo said soberly, "is what's left of New York City."

Blade had never seen anything like it in all his journeys from the Home. He'd encountered ravaged towns and cities, dozens of them. But he'd never been this close to a city struck by a thermonuclear device, and the impression was instantly seared into his mind's eye. The material he'd read about World War III, the many stories he'd heard over the years, even knowing the mutants and the mutates were by-products of the conflict, none of it had prepared him for . . . this!

How could it?

Even here, even 20 miles from the heart of New York City, the devastation was awesome. Every building in sight, every former residence or office structure or retail establishment, had been destroyed. Most were mere piles of litter and debris. A few retained one wall, a small minority two walls. It looked as if a gigantic windstorm, a tremendous cyclone of inconceivable magnitude, had ripped into every building and literally blown them apart.

"It got to me the first time I saw it," Captain Wargo confided.

Blade tore his eyes from the desolation. "Got to you?" You never mentioned being here before."

"Once," Wargo confirmed. "Shortly before I entered the Civilized Zone to find your Family. I was here on a reconnaisance mission for the Minister."

"How far did you go?" Blade asked.

"This far," Wargo said. "But I was told it gets worse

the further we go."

"How could it get worse?" Geronimo wondered aloud.

"There's one way to find out," Blade said. He looked up at a control panel imbedded in the roof above his head. The SEAL's Operations Manual had been explicit in detailing the proper operation of the control panel. Unfortunately, he'd never had the occasion to test the instructions. Plato had been reluctant to operate the SEAL in the amphibious mode. What if it sank? he had speculated to the assembled Family. They could not afford to lose the transport, and their timid attitude had restrained them from verifying if the vehicle could function on water as well as land.

Now they had no choice.

Blade reached up and flicked a silver toggle switch. He waited a few seconds until he detected an audible "thunk" from underneath the carriage. With painstaking care, his nerves on edge, he slowly eased the SEAL down the bank to the edge of the river, then braked.

"What are you waiting for?" Captain Wargo demanded.

"We could all end up at the bottom of the Hudson," Blade commented.

Captain Wargo drew his pistol. "And where do you think you'll wind up if you don't keep going?"

Blade shifted his right foot to the accelerator, gently applying pressure.

The SEAL slid into the river.

Blade quickly raised his right hand and deftly punched two buttons. For a moment nothing happened, but then the SEAL bucked in the water and a loud clunking emanated from the rear of the transport.

"What's happening?" Captain Wargo asked nervously.

"I closed the wheel ports before we entered the Hudson," Blade replied. "The tires have just retracted and been elevated above the water line. That clunk you heard was the outboard dropping from under the storage section."

"What's next?" Wargo inquired.

"Just this," Blade said, and flicked a second toggle switch.

From behind and under the SEAL came a muted sputtering and metallic coughing, followed by a steady throbbing.

"Hey! The water back here is churning!" the soldier in the rear of the SEAL yelled.

"Is that the outboard motor?" Captain Wargo asked.

"What do you think?" Blade answered.

The SEAL was moving forward, plowing through the water, bearing due east.

Blade turned the steering wheel, gratified when the bulky transport angled to the south.

"We did it!" Captain Wargo said, elated. "The thing is working! Nothing will stop us now!"

"Aren't you forgetting the Zombies?" Geronimo remarked.

"The Zombies!" Wargo snorted. "We'll make mincemeat out of them. Here. Let me show you." He motioned at the trooper in the rear, and the soldier lifted an automatic rifle from the pile of supplies and passed it to the front.

Geronimo's eyes widened when he saw the gun.

Captain Wargo took the piece and hefted it in his hands. "Have you ever seen a beauty like this?"

Blade glanced to the right, getting his first good glimpse of the automatic rifle. He nearly betrayed his bewilderment. The gun was a carbon copy of the one taken from the man caught spying by the Moles. The same 20-inch barrel and folding stock, the same short silencer and elaborate scope, the same 30-shot magazine.

"Is something wrong?" Captain Wargo asked suspiciously.

"No. Why?" Blade responded.

"I don't know." Wargo shrugged. "Nothing, I guess." He stroked the rifle. "Isn't this a beauty?"

"Where did you get it?" Blade innocently inquired.

"We manufacture them, of course," Captain Wargo

said. "They are standard gear for every Technic soldier. They're state-of-the-art, as far as automatics go. Called the Dakon II. They fire four-hundred-five grain fragmentation bullets. They'll drop anything!" he boasted.

"Including Zombies, I hope?" Geronimo chimed in.

"Including Zombies," Captain Wargo declared. He tapped the small plastic panel on one side of the rifle, near the stock. "This is a digital readout. Lets you know exactly how many rounds you have left in the gun—"

"Is that because Technic soldiers can't count without using their fingers and toes?" Geronimo asked, interrupting.

Wargo ignored the taunt. "See these four buttons here? The first button activates the digital counter. The second is for full automatic, the third for semiautomatic. The fourth button ejects your spent magazines."

"What's the fifth button for?" Blade queried. "The one on top of the scope?"

Captain Wargo chuckled. "I told you this was the ultimate in killing power. The button on the scope activates the Laser Sighting Mode."

"It's a laser too?" Blade asked in amazement. He'd read a little about lasers in the Family science classes. Laser technology had been extensively employed prior to the Big Blast.

"Not in the way you mean," Captain Wargo said. "You see this four-inch tube projecting from the top of the scope? It generates a red light, a laser if you will, and this shows up on your targets as a red dot."

"Red dots?" Blade repeated questioningly.

"Yeah. When you see a red dot on your target, that's precisely where your gun is aimed. So to hit the spot you want, all you have to do is raise or lower the red dot to the point you want," Wargo explained.

"It must take the challenge out of aiming," Geronimo noted.

"You don't need to aim with these," Captain Wargo stated. "The Dakon II does everything for you."

"Does it wipe your derriere after you're done?" Geronimo cracked.

Captain Wargo was about to reply when he paused, gawking at the stark vista ahead.

Blade had seen it too. The SEAL was continuing on its course, staying well to the center of the Hudson River, cleaving the water smoothly as it sailed on a southerly bearing into the depths of New York City.

If "city" was the right word.

Any vestige of the former metropolis was gone. The demolished homes and other buildings had given way to a scene culled from a demented nightmare. The ground was parched, scorched, the earth a reddish tint. Vegetation was completely absent. Piles of twisted, molten slag were everywhere. Small piles. Huge piles. Isolated metal girders still stood here and there, like blackened steel trees amidst hills of melted structures.

Blade scanned both sides of the Hudson, astonished. From his schooling days at the Home, he knew New York City had once been inhabited by millions of people. Something like 15 or 20 million when the war broke out. He could scarcely conceive of every one of them, millions upon millions, being reduced to smoking ashes in a matter of seconds. Crisped to nothing in the space of a heartbeat. The very idea was mind-boggling.

"How could they do this to themselves?" Geronimo inquired absently.

"They were idiots," Captain Wargo said.

"Is that it? Is that the only answer?" Geronimo asked.

"What more do you need?" Captain Wargo encompassed both banks with a wave of his hand. "What else would you call someone who would do this? They were fools, because they possessed great power and they didn't know how to use it."

"What do you mean?" Geronimo queried.

"If the Americans had been smart," Wargo stated, "they would have thrown everything they had at the Soviets without warning."

"What?"

"I'm right and you know it," Captain Wargo said. "The Americans blew their chance by letting the Soviets catch up to them. The Americans developed a nuclear capability first. They should have used it before anyone else did the same and conquered the world."

"You're putting me on," Geronimo declared.

"I am not," Captain Wargo responded. "You have a huge library at your Home. You must be familiar with American history."

"We studied it," Geronimo said.

"Right. Then you know what happened to the Americans. They let the Soviets produce their own nuclear arsenal, until it reached the point where neither side had a distinct advantage over the other. And look at what it got them! Mutual destruction. No, the Americans would have been wiser to launch a war before the Soviets built their first nuclear weapon. They could have conquered the globe in weeks and saved themselves a lot of trouble in later years." He paused. "Patton was right all along."

"Patton?" Geronimo reiterated.

"An American general during World War II," Wargo said. "He was all for putting the Russians in their place. He never trusted them. But the civilian leaders refused to subscribe to his opinions. They should have listened to him."

"I'm curious," Blade spoke up.

"About what?" Wargo replied.

Blade focused on the river, watching for floating logs or other obstacles. "I'm curious about the Technics. Do you consider yourselves Americans?"

"No."

"You don't?"

"Why should we?" Captain Wargo asked. "America is a thing of the past. They had their opportunity and they blew it. It's up to us, the Technics, to forge a new world from the rubble the Americans left as their legacy. And you can be certain we won't commit the same boneheaded blunders they did!"

"The Technics have it all planned out, huh?" Blade casually commented.

"You bet your ass we do," Captain Wargo stated proudly. "Why, by the time we're through everyone in North America will—" He abruptly paused, glancing at the giant Warrior in consternation. "Very clever," he said. "Very clever indeed."

"I don't know what you're talking about," Blade stated.

"Sure you don't," Wargo said, grinning. He gazed out at the expanse of river before them. "Let's change the subject. Why don't you give me a rundown on the SEAL's armaments."

"Again?" Blade asked.

"Humor me," Wargo directed. "I'll need to know what to do in case something happens to you." He smiled wickedly. "Not that we would want anything to happen to you, of course."

"Of course." Blade pointed at a row of silver toggle switches in the center of the dashboard. "Those switches engage our offensive weaponry. They're labeled from left to right with an M, S, F, and R. The M stands for the pair of fifty-caliber machine guns we have hidden in recessed compartments under each front headlight. When you flick the M switch, a metal plate slides upward and the guns automatically fire. The S is for Surface-to-Air Missile, a Stinger mounted on a rack in the roof above the driver's seat. A panel slides aside when the switch is pressed and the Stinger is launched. Our Stingers have an effective range of ten miles, and they're heat-seeking."

"And what about the F and R?" Captain Wargo prompted.

"The F is for the flamethrower positioned at the front of the SEAL, behind the front fender, in the center. Press the F and a portion of the fender lowers, the nozzle of the flamethrower extends six inches, and the flame spurts about twenty feet. The SEAL must not be moving when the flamethrower is used, or you run the risk of an explosion. Finally, we have the R switch. It's for the Rocket Launcher secreted in the middle of the front grill. There you have it."

Captain Wargo was grinning like a kid with a new toy. "Marvelous! Simply marvelous! There's no way the Zombies will stop us now!"

"Says you," Geronimo said.

"They won't be able to stop the SEAL like they did some of our jeeps and trucks," Captain Wargo predicted.

"Aren't you forgetting one little fact?" Geronimo queried.

"What fact?" Wargo responded, shifting in his seat.

"If memory serves," Geronimo reminded the Technic, "you told us some of your teams didn't reach the site of the underground vault. But some did, didn't they? And you said the last word you received was to the effect they were going underground. Am I right?"

"You're right," Wargo conceded grudgingly.

"So the real danger isn't in reaching the site of the New York branch of the Institute of Advanced Technology," Geronimo said. "The true threat comes when we leave the SEAL and descend to the underground vault. Correct?"

Captain Wargo looked worried. "That's true," he admitted.

"Typical white man," Geronimo said to Blade. "He gets all excited because we may reach the spot in one piece where raving cannibals are waiting to rip us apart and eat us for supper." He sighed. "How *did* your race ever defeat mine?"

"Beats me," Blade said, and laughed.

The SEAL was steadily continuing its southerly course. On both sides of the Hudson River utter desolation prevailed.

"There!" the Technic commando in the rear of the transport shouted. "I see something!"

Everyone glanced to the right, in the direction he indicated.

"I don't see anything," Captain Wargo said after a bit.

"I saw something," the soldier insisted.

"Are you sure, Kimper?" Wargo asked doubtfully.

"I'm positive, sir," Private Kimper stated. "I saw something moving."

Blade scanned the mounds of slag, dirt, dust, and rubble. The inhospitable, bleak land seemed to reek of death. "What would be moving out there?" he idly inquired.

"Only one thing," Captain Wargo said. "The Zombies."

"What do you know about these Zombies beside the fact they're cannibals?" Geronimo asked the officer.

"Not much," Wargo confessed. "We know there are thousands of them, and they eat anything they can get their grimy hands on. We also know they live in a maze of underground tunnels, old sewer and electrical conduit systems, not to mention the subway network."

"Thousands of them?" Geronimo stared at the wreckage. "How can they find enough to eat, enough to support so many?"

Captain Wargo shrugged. "They find a way." He thoughtfully chewed on his lower lip, then spoke. "And remember. We have reason to believe the Zombies aren't the only . . . things . . . down there. So when we descend to the vault, watch yourselves."

"I didn't know you cared," Geronimo joked.

"I couldn't care less about what happens to you," Wargo said. "But the Minister wants the SEAL returned to Technic City intact, and you two know more about it than I do. I know I could drive it, but I don't have the extensive experience Blade has accumulated. It would be better for our mission if one of you survives to drive the SEAL back."

"We'll do our best," Geronimo mentioned.

Blade cleared his throat. "How far down is this vault?"

"Far," Wargo said.

"How far, exactly?" Blade inquired.

"Fifteen stories underground," Wargo answered.

"Oh? Is that all?" Blade said facetiously.

"Fifteen floors, with Zombies dogging our heels every step of the way?" Geronimo chuckled. "Sounds like fun."

Captain Wargo picked up a map from the console between the bucket seats. He unfolded the map and consulted the coordinates, then looked up and pointed. "Do you see that?"

Spanning the Hudson ahead was the skeletal framework of an ancient bridge. The central section was gone, and the supports and ramp on the east bank were a mass of pulverized scrap, but the segment on the west bank, bent but intact, served to reveal the purpose of the construction.

"That, if my calculations are correct, was once called the Tappan Zee Bridge," Captain Wargo informed them. "We're getting close to our goal."

The SEAL puttered forward, its powerful outboard maintaining a sustained speed of fifteen knots.

Blade thought of his wife and child, Jenny and Gabriel, and wished he was with them instead of on this insane quest. He wondered how Hickok was faring in the hands of the Technics, and whether the gunman was even alive. If the Technics killed the gunfighter, he would personally insure they paid for the act. So far, in the constricted confines of the SEAL, he'd been unable to make a break for it. But, if Wargo supplied Geronimo and him with firearms, Blade was determined to dispatch the soldiers and head for Technic City. One opening was all it would take, one brief instant when the troopers were diverted by something else. Like a Zombie, perhaps. Blade almost hoped the cannibals would attack.

"Make for the east bank," Captain Wargo curtly ordered.

Blade turned the wheel, bearing toward the eastern bank.

"We should see a small hill," Captain Wargo said, his nose pressed to his window. "There! Do you see it?"

"I see it," Blade said. He surveyed the bank for any hint of movement. The SEAL bounced as it cruised toward the bank, a rhythmic up and down motion caused by the small waves on the Hudson and welling of the water the transport diplaced.

Captain Wargo looked at Private Kimper. "Pass out our helmets," he directed.

Kimper handed a helmet to each Technic soldier.

"Don't we get one?" Blade asked.

"When we reach the site," Wargo said.

"What about guns?" Blade inquired.

"What about them?"

"Do Geronimo and I get one?" Blade asked hopefully.

"Don't make me laugh!" Captain Wargo rejoined.

"But a while ago you said you want one of us to drive the SEAL to Technic City," Blade said.

"I do," Wargo confirmed. "Don't you worry. My men will look after you."

"I hope they do a better job than your other teams have done in dealing with the Zombies," Blade stated.

The SEAL was 20 yards from the bank.

Blade reached up and flicked the appropriate switch to shut down the outboard motor. The throbbing sound abated. Carried forward by its momentum and the flow of the river toward the bank, the transport kept going. Quickly, Blade ran his fingers over the control panel, securing the outboard and opening the wheel ports so the huge tires could assume their usual position.

The SEAL slowly approached the east bank. The tires crunched into the riverbed ten yards from shore.

Blade tramped on the accelerator and the transport wheeled from the Hudson River onto the bank.

"Go straight," Captain Wargo instructed the Warrior.

Blade cautiously drove into the ravaged remains of New York City. He checked his window to insure it was up and locked, then verified Wargo's was also secure. Being this close to the wretched ruins was strange, like driving on an alien planet. Oddly, a cloud of red dust hung suspended in the air, cloaking the city in a mysterious shadow. Some of the molten mounds were several stories high, others squat knolls on the ground. He couldn't determine where the streets and avenues had once been located. Everything was sort of welded together, fused by the intense heat of the thermonuclear blast.

"Keep going straight," Wargo said.

"I'm glad you know where we're going," Blade remarked.

Each of the Technic commandos was now armed with a Dakon II and wearing a camouflage helmet.

Blade noticed a clear plastic area on the front of the helmet, and small holes dotting the helmet area covering their ears. "It looks like your helmets are as elaborate as your guns," he commented.

"They are," Captain Wargo affirmed, keeping his eyes on the fantastic landscape. "Each one is outfitted with a lamp," and he tapped the clear plastic on the front of his helmet, "and sensitive microphones imbedded in the ear flaps. They amplify all sound, giving us superhuman hearing. Nothing can sneak up on us, catch us unawares.

"I trust the Zombies know that," Geronimo said.

"Speaking of the Zombies," Wargo mentioned, "where the hell are they? We should have seen them by now."

"Count your blessings," Geronimo declared.

The SEAL was going deeper and deeper into the ruins.

Blade fidgeted in his seat. He didn't like this one bit. Wargo had a point. Where were the blasted Zombies?

"That's it!" Captain Wargo yelled, leaning forward. "Stop there!"

Their destination was easy to spot. It was the only parking lot in the city. Three jeeps and four trucks were parked near a gaping hole in the ground.

"Those are the vehicles our other teams used," Captain Wargo detailed.

"Why didn't the Zombies drive them off?" Blade asked.

"The Zombies don't have brains enough to come in out of the rain," Wargo replied. "They wouldn't know what to do with those vehicles."

"What about the Soviets?" Geronimo inquired. "They'd drive them off if they found them."

"If they found them," Wargo agreed. "But our intelligence indicates the Russians never enter New York City. And why should they? Do you see anything here worth risking your life for? They're not stupid."

"What does that make us?" Blade wondered aloud. He eased the SEAL in a tight circle, drawing as near to the hole as he could. The closer, the better! The less ground to cover, the fewer Zombies they'd encounter. He braked the SEAL and stared at Wargo. "What next?"

"Stop the engine," Captain Wargo ordered.

"If you say so," Blade said, sighing, and turned the keys in the ignition.

After the sustained whine of the prototypical engine, the abrupt silence was oddly unsettling.

Captain Wargo stared at each of his men. "We've rehearsed this again and again. We'll make it in and out again if we play it by the numbers. Remember. You're the best of the best! Technic commandos! We never fail!"

Blade gazed at the three jeeps and four trucks, but kept his mouth closed.

Captain Wargo glanced at Private Kimper. "Hand me the extra helmets."

Two helmets were forwarded to the officer.

Wargo gave one of the helmets to Blade, the second to Geronimo.

"What am I supposed to do with this?" Geronimo asked. "Grow plants in it?"

"Wear it," Wargo said. "It could save your life. Each helmet contains a miniaturized communications circuit, what we call a Com-Link. We can keep in constant touch without having to shout. Everything you say will be picked up, overheard by the rest of us."

"I hope I don't burp," Geronimo quipped.

Captain Wargo turned to Blade. "What is this guy? The Official Family Comedian?"

"It's a tossup between Geronimo and Hickok," Blade replied.

"Well, I don't want anyone talking unless I give them an order," Captain Wargo instructed them.

"There is one thing I would like to bring up," Geronimo said.

"What is it?" Wargo impatiently snapped.

"I never did get a potty break," Geronimo reminded him. "If I don't go right now, I'll burst."

"Damn. I forgot," Captain Wargo said. "All right. Everyone will exit the SEAL and form at the front.

Blade, be sure the doors are locked and pocket the keys. I want you to stay close to me during this operation. Everyone ready?''

Wargo's men nodded.

"Okay. First, check your Com-Link. Do you see those two buttons under the helmet lamp?'' Wargo said for the benefit of the two Warriors. "Press the one on the right for the Com-Link, and the one on the left for the lamp. But don't flash your lamp until we enter the hole. I don't want you draining your helmet batteries.''

Blade and Geronimo each donned a camouflage helmet and pressed the Com-Link button.

"Can you hear me?'' Captain Wargo asked.

Blade could hear Wargo's voice in his left ear. "I can hear you on the left,'' he responded.

"Me too,'' Geronimo added.

"Perfect. The right ear is your amplifier for detecting the tiniest noise. You'll find the control knob for it on your right ear flap. But wait until we're down below to use it. Got it?'' Wargo questioned them.

"Got it,'' Blade said.

"Ditto,'' came from Geronimo.

"Okay.'' Captain Wargo clutched his Dakon II and took a deep breath. "Here we go.''

The six men hurriedly bailed out of the SEAL. Blade verified the doors were locked. The three Technic soldiers under Wargo's command were professionals; they deployed in a skirmish line around the front of the SEAL, their Dakon IIs at the ready.

"Alright,'' Captain Wargo said. "Our first squad opened this passage leading to the underground vault. We go in one at a time, single file, Kimper on the point. Do you have the scanner?''

"Affirmative,'' Kimper replied, waving a device strapped to his right wrist.

"Then we're all set,'' Captain Wargo said.

"You're forgetting something again,'' Geronimo stated.

Captain Wargo, preoccupied with their impending descent to the exclusion of all else, stared at Geronimo in confusion.

Geronimo placed his right hand on his gonads and jiggled his pants up and down.

"All right!" Wargo snapped. "Go!"

Geronimo unzipped his green pants, then paused. "Well?"

"Well, what?" Captain Wargo demanded.

"Aren't you going to turn around?" Geronimo asked.

"Turn around? Turn around!" Captain Wargo cried in extreme annoyance. "What are you, bashful or something? We've all seen a pecker before, you dimwit!"

"Not my pecker," Geronimo said, and moved off to the left, near one of the abandoned trucks. He turned his back to the Technics and commenced relieving himself, grateful for the opportunity at long last. He'd had to go so bad his testicles had ached.

Blade grinned at the anger on Wargo's face. He shifted his attention to the large hole not ten feet away. A pile of metal, stones, bricks, and other rubble was stacked behind the hole. Evidently, the first Technic squad on the scene had spent hours uncovering the shaft.

"Activate your scanner," Captain Wargo directed Private Kimper.

Blade watched as Kimper pressed a button and turned several knobs on the black device attached to his right wrist. The scanner was rectangular, with a lot of dials and switches and a grid-laced plastic template.

"Calibrated, sir," Kimper announced.

"Anything?" Wargo queried anxiously.

"Just us," Private Kimper responded.

Blade glanced at his fellow Warrior. Geronimo was still saturating the dust at his feet with a steady stream of urine, a happy grin creasing his features.

"Hurry it up!" Wargo barked.

"Some things can't be rushed," Geronimo retorted.

Blade placed his hands on his hips, wishing he had his Bowies. But the Technics had refused to bring them. His prized knives and Commando and Geronimo's tomahawk, FNC, and Arminius were all in Technic City. The prospect of confronting carnivorous humanoid mutations without weapons was singularly distasteful. He could only pray the Technics knew what they were doing.

"All done," Geronimo said, zipping his pants. He examined the nearest slag mounds and ruins. Great Spirit, preserve them! He fervently craved a weapon, any weapon. The Zombies had to be lurking out there, somewhere. He contemplated the likelihood of being injured, or worse, and dreaded the idea. The last time he'd been hurt was in Catlow, Wyoming, when he'd been shot twice. Once in the head, a surface scratch, and once in the left shoulder. He'd mistakenly assumed his collarbone was broken, but it turned out the bullet had only penetrated the flesh near the collarbone. Still, the discomfort and pain had lingered for months, requiring consummate concentration on his part to prevent the injury from temporarily incapacitating him. All of the Warriors were required to take a course taught by a Family Elder entitled "The Mental and Spiritual Mastery of Pain." But even with such training, sometimes it was hard to—

What was that?

Geronimo tensed. He'd distinctly detected a faint scratching.

"Something!" Private Kimper suddenly shouted, focused on his pulse scanner.

"What is it?" Captain Wargo asked.

"Now it's gone!" Private Kimper said. He was young, inexperienced in combat, and scared out of his wits.

"Keep scanning," Captain Wargo commanded. He began to doubt the wisdom of bringing Kimper on the mission. But Kimper, amazingly, had friends in high places, and one of those "friends" was influential with the Minister. No less a personage than Arthur Ferguson had personally requested to have Kimper taken on the mission. Ferguson knew what success would mean to Kimper's career.

"There it is again!" Kimper exclaimed. "But I don't get it! The images keep fading in and out. How can they do that?"

Captain Wargo frowned. How could they indeed? They might, if the life-forms were continually passing between a solid object or objects containing steel and the scanner.

"The reading is getting stronger!" Kimper warned them.

"How many do you read?" Captain Wargo asked.

Private Kimper glanced at his superior, his skin pale. "It's off the scale!"

Geronimo, momentarily distracted by Wargo and Kimper, heard another scraping noise. He turned, perplexed, because all he could see was rubble and the abandoned jeeps and trucks.

The abandoned jeeps and trucks!

"They're here!" Geronimo yelled in alarm, even as a macabre form hurtled from the cab of the nearest truck directly toward him and a horde of repellant apparitions charged from the gloom of the benighted hole.

12

He almost had it!

Only an inch to go!

Hickok strained against the manacles binding his wrists, his sinewy muscles rippling, his shoulders corded knots, sweat coating his skin and blood dribbling down his wrists. It'd taken two days, two days of strenuous effort, secretly exerting himself to the maximum whenever the chamber was empty. Fortunately, a guard only checked on him four times a day, and he always announced his arrival by rattling his keys as he unlocked the door. Twice daily the guard would bring a tray of food and feed the prisoner.

And, by Hickok's reckoning, it was close to feeding time.

The gunman grunted and groaned as he wrenched his arms from side to side, twisting his wrists back and forth, torturously endeavoring to free his arms.

He could do it!

Hickok knew his escape was only a matter of time. Sooner or later, if he could maintain his frantic contortions, the combination of sweat and blood would provide the lubrication necessary for his wrists to slide from the manacles.

But could he do it before the guard arrived?

He must, the gunman told himself. Otherwise, the guard might notice the ring of crimson around his wrists.

He had to do it *Now!*

Hickok's hair was plastered to his head, drops of

sweat dripping from his chin, as he toiled at his task, his chest heaving from his laborious exertion. His eyes roamed about the room and settled on the white plastic bucket at his feet.

The bastards wouldn't even unlock the manacles and permit him to relieve himself!

They'd pay!

Dear Spirit, *how* they'd pay!

Hickok's mouth curved downward, exposing his grit teeth as he grimaced in agony.

It felt as if his arms were being torn from their sockets!

Hickok savagely jerked his right arm.

Come on!

With a pronounced squishing sound, the gunman's right wrist popped loose of the steel manacle restraining his arm. The momentum swung him around in a circle, tearing at the tendons in his left shoulder as his body sagged.

Bingo!

Hickok reached up and clasped the right manacle, still imbedded in the wall. Using the manacle for support, he pulled his left wrist free in moments.

Just as keys jangled at the door.

Perfect timing! Hickok gripped the left manacle, then drooped his body and lowered his chin, assuming his usual resigned position. A smile touched the corners of his mouth.

Now he was ready.

Let the son of a bitch come!

The guard entered the chamber, a tray of food in his right hand, his keys in his left. He wore a camouflage uniform, black boots, and an automatic pistol attached to his green web belt.

Hickok, feigning dejection, glanced up.

The guard, a solidly built soldier in his forties with brown hair and brown eyes, closed the door. "Well, how's our hick doing today?"

Hickok didn't respond. He was accustomed to being baited; the guards took perverted delight in amusing themselves at his expense.

The trooper advanced toward the gunman. "What's wrong with you? Antisocial or something?"

Hickok didn't answer.

The guard stopped in front of the gunman and stared at his weary face. "You look awful, stupid. Are you getting your beauty rest?" He cackled at his joke.

Hickok's blue eyes darted over the food tray. A glass of juice. A plate containing potatoes and a slice of meat. One fork and one knife, a dull butter knife from the looks of it. Not much, but it would have to do.

"You'd best enjoy this meal," the trooper was saying. "I've heard through the grapevine you don't have too many meals left."

Hickok's interest was piqued. "Why's that?" he asked.

"Ahhh! You are alive!" the guard cracked. "Do you really want to know?" he taunted the Warrior.

"You're the one who brought it up," Hickok said. "You probably didn't hear a thing."

"I did so!" the trooper said indignantly.

"Yeah. Sure."

"Think you know it all, don't you, smart-ass?" the Technic said.

"I know more than you."

"Is that so? Did you know the Minister plans to rack your ass after your buddies return from New York City?" the guard gloated.

"Nope," Hickok admitted. "I didn't know that."

The soldier smirked.

"But I know something *you* don't know," Hickok mentioned nonchalantly.

"Like what?" the guard demanded.

"I don't think you'd want to know," Hickok said.

"You tell me or I'll cram this food down your throat!" the soldier stated. His gaze fell on the white plastic bucket. "Better yet, I'll dump your shitpail on your head!"

"Are you sure you want to know?" Hickok asked, tensing.

"I want to know!" the Technic persisted.

Hickok shrugged. "If you insist." He lunged, his left

hand grasping the guard's shirt and yanking him off balance as his right streaked to the fork and grabbed the implement.

Completely startled, the Technic dropped the tray and the keys, the tray clattering as it struck the floor. He tried to pull away, but the gunman's left hand was locked on his shirt. The Warrior's upper torso, without the shackles securing the wrists to suspend it, pressed down on the guard, causing his knees to sag.

Hickok touched the fork tines to the guard's right eye. "Make one move and you're blinded for life!" he threatened harshly.

The guard gulped.

"Do exactly as I say or I'll ram this fork into your eye!" Hickok growled.

"What . . . what do you . . . want?" the trooper stammered.

"Reach down slowly, and I mean *slowly*, with your right hand and remove your pistol from your holster. Do it slow! One false move and you know what I'll do!"

"Yes," the guard stated in abject fright. He could feel the metal tines digging into his right eyelid.

"Use only your thumb and forefinger to draw the gun!" Hickok directed. "Lift it—slowly—up to me!"

The guard trembled as his right hand lowered to the holster flap and undid the snap. He carefully eased his thumb and forefinger under the leather flap and withdrew the pistol, holding it by the grips.

"Slowly!" Hickok said.

The Technic licked his dry lips as he moved in slow motion, raising the automatic to chest level, inches from Hickok's left hand.

"A little higher," Hickok instructed him.

The guard elevated the pistol to within an inch of the gunman's right hand.

Hickok glanced at the automatic, a 45 of indeterminate manufacture, probably produced by the Technics. He saw a safety button above the grips.

Blast!

The safety was on!

Hickok hesitated. He would need to drop the fork,

grab the pistol, and flick the safety all in one move, leaving himself vulnerable for the fraction of a second his right hand would be empty. Could he do it before the soldier reacted?

Was there any other option?

"You've been a good boy," Hickok said sarcastically. "But I still think I should put out your eye!"

"Please!" the trooper whined. "Don't!"

Hickok scraped the fork tines over the guard's right eyelid, and the soldier flinched, his eyes closing in instinctive defense as his face recoiled.

Which was just what the gunman wanted.

Hickok released the fork and snatched the automatic, his thumb flipping the safety off, and before the Technic quite knew what had transpired he found the fork replaced by the pistol. "Now we come to the easy part," Hickok said.

"Anything," the guard declared.

"Your momma sure raised a polite cuss," Hickok joked. "Oh. Sorry. I forgot. You Technic types don't know who your momma or pappa was, do you?"

"No," the trooper replied.

"Too bad. A little parental love might have changed you from a jackass to a thoroughbred." Hickok wagged the pistol barrel downward. "Now I want you to lower us down, real slow. I'll let you kow when to stop."

Struggling to support the gunman's weight, the soldier eased to his knees.

"I'm gonna let go of your shirt," Hickok said. "When I do, slide your butt backwards. Don't try anything stupid!"

The trooper nodded his understanding.

Hickok released his hold on the shirt, shoving the guard from him and dropping his left hand to the tiled floor to support his body. He wound up in the push-up position, his left arm bracing him, his ankles smarting like the dickens from the manacles above his feet.

The Technic was crouched not a foot away, staring at the pistol barrel.

"Pick up the keys," Hickok ordered.

The trooper immediately complied, stretching his left

arm to the keys and cautiously retrieving them.

"Now unlock my legs," Hickok said. "I'll have you covered all the way, and believe me when I say I can perforate your noggin if you so much as look at me crossways. Do it!"

The guard sidled to the left, still on his knees, toward the wall.

Hickok shifted his left arm, twisting his body, keeping the pistol in his right hand trained on the trooper.

The soldier reached the wall and quickly unfastened the first manacle.

Hickok felt a wave of relief as the agony in his left leg subsided.

The guard unlocked the last manacle.

Hickok rolled to his right, coming up on his knees, the automatic pointed at the Technic. "Thanks, pard. Now stand up and lock the manacles on yourself."

The soldier obeyed without complaining, securing his legs and left wrist.

"Now freeze!" Hickok said.

The Technic became a statue.

Hickok rose and walked up to the guard, placing the pistol barrel a centimeter from the soldier's nose. "Blink, and you'll wind up with a new nasal passage!"

The trooper's throat bobbed.

Hickok locked the right steel manacle on the guard's right wrist, then smiled. "Do you want to live?"

The Technic nodded.

"Then tell me where the blazes they've got my guns and clothes," Hickok directed.

"Right here," the guard responded.

"Here?" Hickok scanned the chamber. All he saw was the brown easy chair. He tapped the barrel on the Technic's nose. "You wouldn't be joshin' me, would you?"

"No!" the soldier assured the gunman. He nodded toward the right-hand wall. "There! You'll find them there!"

Hickok stared at the blue wall. "Where?"

"They're in a closet," the trooper said.

"A closet?"

"A compartment in the wall. Go to the center of the wall," the guard stated.

Hickok walked to the middle of the wall, the pistol trained on the trooper. If the wall was booby-trapped, he intended to blow the soldier away before he went.

"Look for a small button," the guard said. "A little circle on the wall."

Hickok recalled the incident with the syringe, and how Captain Wargo had touched a spot on the left wall, exposing the tray. He peered at the seemingly solid wall. "I don't see it."

"Keep looking!" the Technic said nervously. "It's there!" he assured the gunman.

Hickok saw a circular indentation to his right, about waist height. He pressed the indentation and it sank inward several inches. So that's how they did it!

With a whisk of air, a panel slid aside, a section of the wall simply disappearing as it slid into a recessed groove.

"Bingo!" Hickok said, smiling.

The compartment was six feet high by five feet wide. A metal bar was aligned across the space, six inches from the top. Dangling from silver metal hangers were the gunman's buckskin shirt and leggings. His moccasins had been deposited on the floor in a corner. Leaning against the back wall were Hickok's Henry, Blade's Commando, and Geronimo's FNC. Lying in a pile in the middle of the compartment were Blade's Bowies, Geronimo's tomahawk and Arminius, and one other item, the sight of which caused the gunman's eyes to light up and a wave of genuine joy to wash over him: his pearl-handled Colt Python revolvers in their holsters.

Praise the Spirit!

Hickok crouched and laid the Technic pistol on the floor. He drew one of the Pythons and checked the cylinder to insure it was loaded. Satisfied, he raised the revolver and stroked his right cheek with the cool barrel.

The guard was gawking at the gunman in amazement.

"What's the matter?" Hickok demanded gruffly.

"Ain't you ever seen anyone in love with a gun before?"

"You're crazy," the Technic mustered the courage to comment.

"You think so, huh?"

"What else would you call it?" the soldier countered. "I've never seen anybody act the way you do over a rotten gun."

"These Pythons have gotten me out of more tight scrapes than I care to remember," Hickok said. "I know they're just tools of my trade, but after all these years I've sort of developed a personal relationship with 'em. In a fix, they're the best friends I've got."

"Like I said," the guard reiterated, "you're crazy."

"And you talk too much," Hickok rejoined.

The guard clammed up.

Hickok hurriedly dressed, relieved to be clothed again. He strapped his gunbelt around his waist, then paused, considering the other weapons in the closet. What was he supposed to do about them? He couldn't leave them for the Technics. Besides, Blade was as fond of the Bowies and Geronimo as attached to his tomahawk as he was to the Pythons. Nope. He owed it to his pards to take the weapons with him, even if the extra weight slowed him down a mite. He picked up the tomahawk and slid it under his gunbelt in the small of his back. The Bowies, sheaths and all, he angled under the gunbelt, one on either side of the tomahawk. Bending over would pose a problem, but his hands had a clear path to the Pythons. Next, he slung his Henry over his right shoulder. The FNC went over his left. He was about to grab the Commando when he saw the Arminius still on the floor.

Blast!

The gunman unslung the FNC, then draped the Arminius's shoulder holster under his left arm. Finally, he slung the FNC over his left shoulder and took hold of the Commando.

He was ready.

Hickok walked over to the guard.

The Technic blanched. "I did everything you

wanted!" he said, his voice rising.

"And I appreciate it," Hickok remarked. "I surely do. But I'm afraid our friendship has reached the end of the line."

"Are you going to kill me?" the trooper timidly inquired. "I have a wife and son."

Hickok paused, thinking of Sherry and Ringo. "If you care so much for your missus and young'un, what are you doing in the Army?"

"I didn't have any choice," the guard replied.

"Everybody has a choice," Hickok said.

"We don't," the Tecnnic revealed. "We're given tests when we're teenagers, about sixteen. The jobs we're assigned are based on the test results."

"They tell you what kind of work you'll do?" Hickok asked.

The Technic nodded. "We don't have any say in it. They say our system is best because the service we perform for the community, for the common good of all, is based on our demonstrated ability, not on what we might like to do."

"But a person can have talent in more than one field," Hickok noted. "How do they know what'd make you happiest?"

"Make us happy?" The Technic snorted derisively. "Do you know what we're taught? Individual happiness is an illusion," he quoted from memory. "The good of all is the goal of the many. What is best for all brings real happiness."

"So they tested you and told you the Army was going to be your career, whether you liked it or not?" Hickok concluded.

"You got it."

"Pitiful. Just pitiful. Sort of makes me feel sorry for you. So I'll tell you what I'm gonna do. I'm not gonna whack you upside the head like I planned," Hickok said.

"Thanks," the Technic said, manifestly relieved.

"But on the other hand . . ." Hickok crouched and began unlacing the guard's right boot.

"What are you doing?" the Technic asked.

"Hold onto your hat," Hickok said. He removed the boot, then the black sock underneath.

The guard perceived the gunman's intent. "But that sock is dirty!" he protested.

Hickok rose. "Say Ahhhhhh."

"But—"

Hickok raised the Commando in his left hand. "Say Ahhhh."

The Technic opened his mouth wide. "Ahhhh—"

Hickok jammed the sock into the guard's mouth, all the way in. He hastily removed the lace from the black boot, lopped the lace around the guard's face, and tied it tight, the knot situated in the middle of his open mouth to prevent the sock from being spit out. "I reckon that ought to hold you for a spell. Adios."

The gunman crossed to the door. If all went well, he'd find a flight of stairs lickety-split and vacate the Central Core before they realized he was missing. If he could find an unattended jeep or truck in the parking lot, he'd swipe it and make for the western gate.

Yes, sir.

Things were finally going his way.

It was beginning to look like busting out of Technic City would be a piece of cake!

Hickok opened the door and peeked around the jamb. The corridor, white tiles on the floor and walls, yellow panels on the ceiling, was deserted.

Like he said.

A piece of cake.

Hickok stepped into the corridor and closed the door behind him, just as a squad of four Technic soldiers, each armed with an automatic rifle, rounded a corner to his right!

13

The Zombies were walking nightmares.

Each Zombie was naked, its gray flesh pitted and filthy, with peculiar patches of greenish blisters randomly distributed over the body. Their eyes were reddish and unfocused, their mouths gaping maws of yellow, tapered teeth. Although they stood well over six feet in height, they were emaciated, their arms and legs resembling broomsticks.

Geronimo nearly gagged as a putrid stench filled the air. He backpedaled as more Zombies poured from the abandoned vehicles.

Something collided with his back.

Geronimo whirled, and found Blade alongside him. "What do we do?" he asked.

The Technics opened up with their Dakon IIs, their fragmentation bullets tearing into the hissing Zombies and ripping them apart, blowing their chests and skulls to shreds or tearing limbs from their bodies. Greenish fluid sprayed everywhere.

The Zombies never broke stride. Their grisly arms extended, their yellow fingernails glinting in the sunlight, their thin lips quivering in anticipation of their next meal, saliva pouring from their mouths, they advanced on the Technics, row after ravenous row, undeterred even when an arm or leg was shattered by a dumdum bullet. Nothing short of their chest or head exploding into smithereens stopped them.

The thup-thup-thup of the Dakon IIs mixed with the sibilant hissing of the Zombies.

Blade and Geronimo found themselves pressed against the SEAL's grill, the Technics in a ring in front of them, the horde of Zombies beyond.

"What do we do?" Geronimo said in Blade's left ear.

Blade was about to reply when iron-like fingers clasped his legs and he was brutally wrenched to the ground.

One of the Zombies had crawled under the SEAL and grabbed him!

Blade, prone on his back, saw the hunched-over creature about to bite into his left calf. He drew his right foot up and drove it down, catching the Zombie on the chin.

The Zombie blinked once, shook its head, and hissed as it clutched at the Warrior's groin.

Blade reached up, gripped the fender, and tried to haul his body from under the transport.

The Zombie snatched his belt buckle and started pulling the Warrior down, its mouth inches from his thighs.

Private Kimper suddenly appeared, stooped over to the left of Blade, his Dakon II pointed at the Zombie. He pulled the trigger, the Dakon II recoiling as the heavy slugs tore into the Zombie's face.

Blade was spattered by shredded flesh and green mush as the Zombie's head burst apart. A pulpy substance landed on his right cheek. He swiped at the gore and wriggled his shoulders past the fender. Stout hands clasped his armpits and helped draw him to his feet.

"Are you all right?" Geronimo inquired apprehensively.

Blade nodded.

The Technics had dispatched the Zombies hidden in the trucks and jeeps, and were concentrating their fire on the monstrosities flowing from the hole.

"See?" Captain Wargo cried gleefully. "What did I tell you? We can handle these freaks!"

So it appeared. The Zombies disgorging from the hole were becoming fewer and fewer; stacks of their dead covered the ground between the Technics and the underground entrance.

Four more Zombies charged from the dark hole, and were promptly decimated by fragmentation bullets.

Captain Wargo turned to Blade, smirking triumphantly. "These Zombie's aren't so tough! I can't understand why the other squads had so much trouble."

Blade was concerned by Wargo's overconfidence. Overconfidence bred carelessness. "We're just getting started," he reminded the officer. He pointed at the hole. "Who knows what it will be like down there?"

"Let's find out," Captain Wargo said. "Kimper, watch that scanner! Stay near me! Gatti, take the point!"

The oldest trooper nodded and moved to the edge of the black hole.

"Stay close to me," Wargo said to Blade and Geronimo.

"Do we get a gun?" Blade asked.

"I told you before. No," Wargo replied.

"After what just happened?" Blade said.

"No gun," Captain Wargo stressed. "Let's move out! Check your Com-Links! Don't stray!"

Gatti flicked on his helmet lamp and vanished over the brink.

Captain Wargo led the rest to the rim, sidestepping gory Zombie remains all the way. He crouched, turned on his helmet lamp, and stared downward.

Blade and Geronimo joined the officer, activating their own lamps.

Private Gatti was one flight of stairs below them, sweeping the tunnel with his head lamp. "Nothing," he said softly, the word crisply audible to those perched above him, amplifed by their Com-Links.

"Wait for us," Captain Wargo ordered. He stood and started down the stairs.

Blade frowned, exchanged glances with Geronimo, and followed Wargo, Geronimo on his heels and Kimper behind Geronimo.

"Scanner's clean," Kimper said, his eyes glued to the grid.

"Keep me posted," Wargo directed.

They reached the first landing and paused.

Blade's helmet lamp illuminated dusty, cobweb-covered walls and railings. The light from the lamps penetrated 20 feet into the inky gloom; beyond loomed a curtain of ominous black.

"We take the stairs to the bottom," Captain Wargo said. "The vault is near the stairs, so we should be in and out before the Zombies can regroup."

"I hope you're right," Geronimo said. "Those Zombies give me the creeps!"

"No talking!" Wargo snapped. "Move out!"

Gatti headed downward.

"Still nothing," Kimper informed them.

Captain Wargo waved his right arm and resumed their descent.

As they passed landing after landing, six in succession without encountering more Zombies, Blade wondered if Wargo was right after all. Had the Zombies called it quits? The cannibals had taken quite a beating up above; the Dakon IIs had destroyed them in droves. Maybe the Zombies weren't as fierce as their reputation alleged. But if that was the case, then what had happened to the earlier Technic squads?

"Trouble," Private Gatti said from a flight below.

"What is it?" Captain Wargo demanded.

"I think you should see this for yourself, sir," Gatti replied.

The party hastened to the next level.

"See what I mean?" Gatti asked.

"Oh, no!" one of the other troopers complained.

Captain Wargo stared at the problem, dazed.

Blade looked at Geronimo.

"Now what do we do?" Geronimo inquired.

The stairs came to an abrupt termination; jutting struts and bars were suspended in midair, and pieces of debris lined the landing; a heavy steel girder protruded from the north wall, hanging in space; beyond was a stygian void.

"What could have caused this?" Captain Wargo questioned.

"Maybe a little thing like a nuclear war," Geronimo

remarked.

"Do we turn back?" Blade queried the Technic officer.

Captain Wargo shook his head. "No, we don't," he declared obstinately. "The stairs may still be intact farther down."

"And how do we reach them?" Blade asked.

Captain Wargo slowly pivoted, his helmet light playing over the stairs and the surrounding walls. "There must be . . ." He pointed at the west wall. "Look! A door! I knew there'd be one."

"Just our luck," Geronimo groused.

The door was ajar several inches. A faded sign read "STAIRWELL EXIT LEVEL #8."

"Gatti. Point," Captain Wargo directed.

Private Gatti hesitated for a moment, then cautiously pushed the door open. "There's a hallway here," he announced.

"Let's go!" Captain Wargo barked.

Blade detected a visible reluctance in the Technic soldiers. Their pensive features accurately reflected their growing apprehension. And who could blame them? The lower they descended, the more certain they were to encounter more Zombies. He followed Wargo through the doorway, stepping over a skeleton on the floor, a skeleton wearing a dust-covered camouflage helmet. "One of yours?" he asked Wargo.

"Must be," Captain Wargo answered. "I don't see his dog tags, but the helmet is definitely ours."

"The bones were picked clean," Geronimo observed.

"And if you let the Zombies catch you," Captain Wargo said, "the same fate will befall you."

"Do you always look at the cheery side of life?" Geronimo rejoined.

"Captain!" Private Gatti stated from up ahead.

"What is it?" Wargo asked.

"A junction," Gatti replied.

"On our way," Captain Wargo said.

They found Gatti 20 yards further ahead, shielded by the corner of a wall at the junction of two corridors.

"Scanner?" Captain Wargo declared.

Private Kimper studied his pulse scanner. "Faint readings, sir. Almost undetectable. Nothing close."

Wargo pondered for a minute. "Take that branch," he commanded Gatti, indicating the corridor to the left.

The point man took off.

"How do you know which one to take?" Blade inquired.

"I don't," Captain Wargo responded.

They slowly moved down the hallway, their helmets constantly becoming entangled in cobwebs, their feet kicking up puffs of dust with every step.

"May I make a comment?" Geronimo said.

"What is it?" Captain Wargo asked.

"Do you see all these cobwebs we keep bumping into?" Geronimo mentioned.

"Yeah. What about them?"

"So where are all the spiders?" Geronimo commented. "Hundreds of spiderwebs and not one spider. Doesn't that strike you as strange?"

"I never gave it much thought," Wargo admitted.

"Maybe the Zombies eat the spiders," Blade said.

"Yuck," Geronimo stated. "You could be right. The Zombies must have some sort of dietary staple if they're surviving in large numbers. Spiders would be as nutritious as anything else."

A disturbing speculation registered in Blade's mind. "Say, Wargo."

"What?"

"How many Zombies are there in New York City?" Blade inquired.

"I'm not sure," Captain Wargo replied. "Our experts estimate in the neighborhood of four or five thousand. Why?"

"Is that all?"

"Isn't that enough?" Wargo retorted.

"You're missing my point," Blade said. "Only four or five thousand. Why aren't there more of them?"

"How the hell should I know?" Wargo said stiffly. "Why don't you ask the next one you run into?"

"What is your point?" Geronimo wanted to know.

"The Zombies have been here since the Big Blast,

right?'' Blade answered. ''They've had over a century in which to breed. So why aren't there more of them? Only four thousand in one hundred years doesn't seem like much.''

''Maybe they have a hard time getting it up,'' Captain Wargo said.

''Or perhaps there is something else down here,'' Blade noted. ''Something eating the Zombies and keeping their population down.''

''Eating the Zombies?'' Captain Wargo reiterated in disbelief. ''What could possibly do that?''

''Let's hope we don't have to find out,'' Blade declared.

''Captain Wargo!'' It was Gatti.

''What is it?'' Captain Wargo answered.

''I've found a hole in the floor,'' Gatti informed his superior.

''Stay put,'' Wargo ordered.

They reached the point man within a minute, squatting at the rim of a jagged opening in the corridor floor.

''It leads to the floor below,'' Private Gatti told them.

Captain Wargo crouched and peered through the hole. The floor of another corridor was 12 feet below. ''We go down one at a time,'' he instructed them. ''Hang by the arms and drop. You won't have more than six feet or so to fall. Gatti, you first.''

Private Gatti slung his Dakon II over his right shoulder and slid his legs over the edge of the hole.

Captain Wargo leaned down so he could see the hallway below. ''Go ahead. I'll cover you.''

Gatti eased from sight and released his grip. He landed unsteadily, but righted himself instantly, quickly unslinging his Dakon II.

''Cover us,'' Wargo told Gatti. He motioned for the rest to take their turn.

Private Kimper was the next to drop, then Blade and Geronimo. While the two Warriors waited for Wargo and the last soldier to reach the lower level, Blade tapped Geronimo's right shoulder and moved to one side.

Blade turned off his Com-Link, and Geronimo did the same. "We're going to make a break for it," Blade whispered. "The first chance we get."

"What about the Genesis Seeds?" Geronimo said softly.

"I doubt they even exist," Blade murmured. "This whole affair has been fishy from the start."

"Just give the signal," Geronimo stated.

"There will be no signal!" Captain Wargo said sharply, advancing on the Warriors with his Dakon II leveled. "How stupid can you be? Did you think by deactivating your Com-Links I couldn't hear your conversation? You forgot the amplifier on the right side of our helmet. I could hear you fart at one hundred yards!"

"I wish I had some beans," Geronimo quipped.

"If you attempt to escape," Captain Wargo warned them, "we will shoot to kill. We'd prefer to take you back to Technic City with us. But the bottom line, gentlemen, is this: you *are* expendable."

"Now you tell us," Blade said sarcastically.

"Let's move out!" Captain Wargo said.

Gatti moved along the inky corridor until his lamp was lost to view.

Captain Wargo shoved Blade with the barrel of his Dakon. "You two will stay in front of us. Move!"

Blade and Geronimo started forward.

"And switch on your damn Com-Links!" Captain Wargo ordered.

As Blade depressed the correct button, a shrill voice filled his helmet.

"Captain!" Private Kimper needlessly shouted. "Readings, sir!"

"How many?"

"Off the scale! Dozens!"

"At what range?"

"They're on the floor above us!" Kimper answered. "And they're heading for the hole we just came through!"

"On the double!" Wargo instructed them.

They began jogging after the point man.

Even as Gatti's terrified scream blasted their ears.

14

Hickok had seen those automatic rifles before: once at the Home when Plato had displayed the weapon appropriated from the spy slain by the Moles, and again at the fence bordering Technic City in the hands of the guards. He recognized a distinctly lethal armament when he saw one, and finding himself confronted by four troopers ten feet away, each with one of the rifles, he automatically reacted as his years of arduous training and experience dictated: he swept up the Commando and squeezed the trigger.

The corridor rocked to the booming of the Commando, the four soldiers taken unaware by the onslaught, their bodies jerking and writhing as they absorbed the large-caliber slugs. Only one of them uttered a sound, a gurgling screech, as he toppled to the tiled floor.

Time to make tracks!

Hickok whirled and ran, his speed impeded by the combined weight of the guns he was carrying. He saw an elevator ahead and paused, mentally debating. The elevator could be rigged, just like the one before. But it might take a minute or so for more troopers to arrive, and by then he could be far away. Besides, how would they know *he* was using the elevator? It could be any Technic.

Go for it!

The gunman sprinted to the elevator and pressed the down button. He didn't know exactly where he was in the Central Core, but odds were he was on one of the higher floors. How many did the Central Core have? Ten, wasn't it?

The elevator arrived with a loud ping and the doors hissed open.

Hickok ducked inside and examined the control panel. A circular button with an 8 imprinted on it was lit up. That must mean he was on the eighth floor! He stabbed another button, the down button, the one with an arrow pointing straight down, and the elevator doors closed.

So far, so good.

Hickok watched the lights flicker, apprehensive, praying he could reach ground level before the Technics realized he was making a bid for freedom.

The button for the sixth floor came on.

"Can't you go any faster?" Hickok asked aloud, and kicked the door. Why was the blamed contraption dropping so slowly? Was this typical of an elevator? A mare could deliver a foal in the time it was taking the blasted elevator to reach the ground!

The elevator had reached the fourth floor.

"Hurry it up!" Hickok said.

The third floor.

Somewhere in the distance a klaxon wailed.

They were on to him! Someone had sounded the alarm!

Second floor.

Hickok tensed, clutching the Commando. He must ignore the odds against him. So what if he was alone and outnumbered millions to one? So what if the entire Technic Army and Police Force would be after him? He was a Warrior, and Warriors never quit. Never. Ever.

The elevator reached the ground floor and the doors whisked open.

The lobby was crammed with people: soldiers, police in their blue uniforms, government officials, and civilians. Waiting outside the elevator was a Technic officer and one other, a man in a brown uniform with gray hair, blue eyes, and a hefty build. The gunman recognized him as the man from the interrogation room, the one who'd showed up with the Minister!

"Howdy! Guess who?" Hickok said.

The Technic officer was completely confounded, frozen, but the man in brown reacted; his blue eyes widened fearfully and his mouth sagged. "You!" he exclaimed.

"Bingo! You get the prize!" Hickok declared, and fired.

The Commando cut them in two, their chests exploding in a spray of crimson flesh.

Hickok burst from the elevator, heading for the gold doors visible on the other side of the spacious lobby.

A Technic policeman loomed ahead, blocking the gunman's path, clawing at an automatic pistol in the holster on his left hip.

Hickok cut loose, ripping the Technic from his crotch to his sternum.

A woman nearby was screaming her lungs out.

Another woman, with a young girl at her side, stood five yards in front of the racing Warrior, gaping.

Blasted bystanders!

Hickok skirted the pair, weaving and twisting as he ran, the crowd parting to allow his passage.

But not all of them.

Another Technic policeman was standing before the gold doors, pistol in his right hand.

Hickok leaped behind a potted fern as the policeman fired. A high-pitched shriek added to the general din. Hickok rolled to the left, and as he did he saw the little girl he'd bypassed falling to the floor with a hole in her forehead.

The rotten bastard!

Hickok came up on his knees, the Commando pressed to his right shoulder, and pulled the trigger.

The Technic in front of the gold doors was slammed backward by the impact, crunching into the doors and slipping to the floor, leaving a red swath in his wake.

Hickok sprinted to the doors. He paused, kicking the dead Technic in the face, crushing his nose. "I can't abide a lousy shot!" he growled, and pushed on the nearest door.

Nothing happened.

What the blazes! Hickok tried one more time with the same result. What the heck was going on? Why wouldn't the door open? He suddenly recalled Wargo using a button to the left of the doors when they entered the Central Core.

There!

Hickok was to the bank of buttons in an instant.

They weren't marked!

The gunman stabbed the first button on the right.

The doors remained closed.

Blast!

A bullet whined off the doors not six inches away.

Hickok punched the button on the far left.

The gold doors slid open.

Move it! his mind thundered, as he scurried outside. The doors slid closed again as he spun, the Commando bucking, the bullets striking the outside button bank and destroying it in a shower of plastic, metal, and fiery sparks.

Let 'em try and get those doors open now!

Hickok crouched and turned to face the parking lot, shocked by the sight he beheld.

Two dozen Technic police were lined up 15 yards away, at attention, their stunned faces focused on the Warrior. Between the formation of police and the gunman was a solitary jeep, and sitting in the rear of the topless vehicle, his features frozen in horrified shock, evidently paralyzed by the abrupt advent of the Warrior, was the Minister.

For the space of a heartbeat it was as if the tableau were in suspended animation. Hickok was hardly aware of a green truck parked alongside the yellow curb not ten feet to his right, or the squad of Technic commandos 40 yards off and approaching on the run. All he saw, the only object of his concentration, the sum total of his world, was the man responsible for subjecting him to the most acute humiliation he'd ever felt, the callous, egotistical tyrant who'd degraded him, who'd caused him to lose face, as Rikki would say, who'd made him eat crow and reveled in the gunman's debasement: the Minister.

For the space of a heartbeat no one moved.

And then the Minister opened his mouth to shout orders to his assembled men, his personal guard, and all hell broke loose.

Hickok fired, the Commando chattering, and the Minister's eyes and nose dissolved as his face was torn to gruesome shreds.

The Technic police went for their weapons.

The Technic commandos were now 30 yards distant.

Hickok raced toward the parked truck, bent over, presenting as difficult a target as possible, shooting as he ran.

Three of the Technic police hit the pavement, blood gushing from their riddled uniforms.

Hickok reached the truck with bullets chipping at the sidewalk and striking the Central Core. He passed a wide picture window and saw a female civilian on the other side, screaming in terror at the demise of the Minister. At least, he assumed she was screaming. Her mouth was open but no sound was audible.

How could this be?

The gunman could scarcely afford a moment's idle speculation. A trooper appeared around the tailgate of the truck, one of those fancy automatic rifles in his hands.

Hickok dived for the sidewalk as the soldier fired. His knees and elbows were lanced by excruciating agony, pain he ingored as he aimed the Commando and squeezed the trigger.

A distinct click greeted his efforts.

The Commando was empty!

There was no time to reload! Hickok rolled to his left, nearer the truck, his right hand flashing to his holster and the right Colt clearing leather even as the trooper sent a few rounds into the sidewalk to the gunman's right, concrete chips flying in every direction. The Warrior fired as the commando sighted for another shot, fired as the commando staggered backward with a hole where his left eye had been, and fired as the commando crashed to the ground with both eyes gone.

Hickok surged erect, his balance unsteady because of all the extra weapons he was carrying, and he lunged for the only available cover, the cab of the green truck.

A red dot appeared on the door of the truck, inches from his left hand.

A red dot?

The Commando clasped between his thumb and first finger, the gunman grasped at the truck handle as the door was hit, flying metal shards zinging every which way. A sharp piece burned a furrow in his left cheek. He instinctively ducked and whirled, cocking the Python.

A soldier was standing near the jammed gold doors, rifle to his shoulder.

Where the blazes had he come from?

Hickok snapped a shot as a red dot materialized on his chest, and the trooper toppled backwards.

Move!

Hickok wrenched the door open as a female member of the Technic police rounded the front fender with her pistol already out. He fired and she stumbled and crashed into the truck, her pistol clattering on the pavement.

This was no place for Momma Hickok's pride and joy!

The gunman scrambled into the truck, letting the Commando drop to the floor, his anxious gaze roving over the dashboard and locking on a set of keys, one of which was already inserted to the right of the steering column.

Eureka!

Hickok grabbed the keys as the windshield was splintered by a fusillade of gunfire.

The Technics were pouring everything they had at the cab.

Hunched over behind the steering wheel, the gunman turned the key and pumped the accelerator. He recollected the last time he'd driven a truck, from Wyoming to Minnesota, and he tried to remember the proper procedure. He recalled the ignition and the gas pedal, but overlooked one crucial component.

The clutch.

Hickok was taken unawares when the truck abruptly
jerked forward. Something thudded against the grill. A
bullet obliterated the rearview mirror. The truck lurched
ahead like a wobbly drunk, starting forward and
abruptly stopping, again and again, tossing him against
the steering wheel.

What the dickens was wrong?

A bullet penetrated the windshield and thudded into
the seat beside him.

Hickok glanced at the floor and spotted the third
pedal. The first was the gas pedal. And the one on the
left was the brake. But what was the other one?

A slug creased his right shoulder, breaking the skin.

The police and commandos were deploying in a
circle, enclosing the vehicle.

The clutch! That was it! Hickok tramped on the
clutch, grinding the gears as he shifted from first to
second and the truck roared across the parking lot. He
kept his head below the dash as round after round
ripped into the vehicle. The clamor was incredible:
metal whining and glass breaking and people shouting
and the windshield dissolving in a shower of glass.

There was another pronounced thud from the front
of the truck.

Hickok sat up to get his bearings. He was going due
south, the truck heading toward a row of parked trikes.

Not ten feet ahead was a solitary commando, a
woman, down on one knee, shooting at the truck engine
in an attempt to disable it.

Hickok floored the accelerator and the truck
lumbered forward. He saw the commando's mouth
open and her petrified eyes widen an instant before
there was a crushing thump and the truck bounced as if
the wheels had encountered a bump.

The passenger-side window blew apart.

Hickok frantically turned the steering wheel, but too
late. The vehicle slewed to the right, its rear end
smashing into the row of trikes and bowling them over.
He spun the wheel again, thundering down an aisle
between the trikes.

A jeep containing three Technic police was zooming

toward him.

Hickok wasn't about to stop. To stop was certain death. The Technics would be on him in a second. He intended to get as far as possible from the Central Core as quickly as possible, and no one or nothing was going to stand in his way.

Especially not one measly jeep!

Hickok's grip on the steering wheel tightened as the truck closed on the jeep. He could see a determined expression on the policeman driving. Obviously, the Technic wasn't about to surrender the right of way.

Thirty feet separated them.

Hickok hunched over the steering wheel and braced for the collision.

Twenty feet.

Would the truck survive the crash? It was a big vehicle, the green trailer it was hauling adding to its bulk, but a wreck at high speed would undoubtedly cripple the motor.

Ten feet.

Hickok held his breath as the two vehicles sped at one another. He flinched in expectation of the impact, and that's when the jeep unexpectedly altered course, swerving to the left and ramming into some trikes.

He'd done it!

Elated, Hickok didn't perceive the danger he posed to the mass of trikes occupying the avenue beyond the parking lot until the truck had jumped a curb and slammed into their midst. Chaos resulted. Screams and shrieks rent the air; battered bodies were flying everywhere; trikes and travelers alike were squashed beneath the huge truck tires, trikes crunching and their drivers and occupants being mashed to a flattened pulp; and random gunshots from the Technic police and the soldiers punctuated the general din.

Blast!

Hickok slammed on the brakes and the truck ground to a rocky halt, the motor idling. He saw dozens of trikes and four-wheelers crash as they wildly endeavored to avoid the melee.

Cries of torment and anguish were voiced by the

injured and dying.

Dear Spirit! What had he done? The gunman vaulted from the cab, landing next to a demolished trike with an elderly man prone over the handlebars. Hickok gaped at the man's vacant brown eyes, appalled by the needless deaths and misery he'd inadvertently caused. To his left was a young boy, lying in a pool of blood. He was shocked to his soul, and the gunman's senses swirled.

He'd killed innocent children!

Children!

A blast from a pistol brought Hickok back to reality. He saw one of the Technic police sighting for a second shot, and whipped his right Colt clear and fired.

The policeman pitched to the tarmac.

Hickok turned, seeking a way out. Six feet away was a lone man seated in an idling four-wheeler, apparently stunned by the destruction, gaping at the Warrior.

Just what he needed!

Hickok jogged to the four-wheeler and shoved the Python barrel into the driver's chest. "Move out!" He climbed into the four-wheeler beside the driver. "Move!"

The driver, a man of 40 with a bald pate and jowly jaws, his green eyes fearfully locked on the Colt, nodded. "Yes, sir!"

"Go!" Hickok goaded him, glancing over his shoulder. The police and soldiers in the parking lot were prevented from reaching him by the gigantic traffic jam blocking the avenue.

The driver of the four-wheeler pulled out, slowly wending his way through the maze of trikes and other vehicles. "Which way?" he asked.

Hickok alertly scanned the avenue for threatening soldiers or Technic police, but the highway ahead was filled with civilians. Very few of them had seen him jump from the truck, but one or two glared at him as he passed.

"Which way?" the driver nervously queried.

"Just keep going," Hickok told him.

"Yes, sir."

The four-wheeler reached an impasse, thwarted by a

veritable wall of vehicles halted by the wreckage and the truck.

"We can't go any further," the driver wailed.

"Yes we can," Hickok said, wagging the Python to the right. "Use the sidewalk. It's not as crowded."

"But that's illegal!" the driver objected.

Hickok rapped the driver on the temple with the Colt. "Take your pick. A spell in the calaboose or a bullet in the brain?"

"Calaboose?"

"The hoosegow," Hickok explained.

"Hoosegow?" the driver repeated, even more confused.

"The jail, dummy!" Hickok snapped.

The driver gingerly wheeled the four-wheeler onto the sidewalk. Shouts and oaths greeted this unprecedented action, but the civilians moved aside at the sight of the blond man in the strange buckskins carrying an arsenal.

Hickok glanced back at the carnage he'd caused. He remembered that little boy, dead, awash in crimson, and he shuddered. He thought of his precious Ringo, and he could vividly imagine the grief the parents of the boy would feel when—

Wait a minute!

That boy didn't have any parents! Not natural ones anyhow. Would his surrogate parents feel the same way a natural parent would?

"What's your name?" Hickok demanded of the driver.

Pale as the proverbial ghost, the heavyset man looked at the gunfighter. "Spencer."

"Do you love your parents?" Hickok asked.

If complete consternation was comical, then the driver was hilarious. But Hickok didn't feel much like laughing.

"My parents?" Spencer said. "You want to know about my parents?"

"Yeah. I know you folks in Technic City ain't raised by your true mom and dad," Hickok stated. "But what about the people who do rear you? Do you love them?"

"Of course not," Spencer responded while circumventing a squat blue box in the middle of the sidewalk marked with the word "MAIL." "You must not be from Technic City if you can ask a stupid question like that. . . ." Spencer's voice trailed off as the enormity of his own idiocy sank home. He'd called this crazy man stupid! What would the lunatic do?

Hickok disregarded the insult. "If you don't love 'em, how do you feel about them?"

"They raise us," Spencer replied. "That's it. Why should we feel anything? Emotion is for simpletons."

The lunatic, amazingly, grinned. "Thanks. I needed that."

Spencer, perplexed, shook his head. "I don't get it."

Hickok waved the Colt. "No. But you will if you don't quit flappin' your gums and pick up speed."

"I'm going as fast as I can," Spencer protested.

Hickok rammed the Python into Spencer's ribs.

The four-wheeler increased its speed.

15

The three soldiers and the pair of Warriors reached the
end of the corridor and came to an abrupt stop.

The hallway was a dead end.

"The Zombies are on our level!" Private Kimper
shouted, the pulse scanner held next to his face.

"We're trapped!" Captain Wargo exclaimed.

Blade surveyed the corridor. There was no sign of
Gatti. Where was he?

"Where's Gatti?" Wargo demanded.

Blade ran, retracing their steps. He reached an open
doorway on the right and peered inside, his helmet lamp
revealing the interior. It was a room, perhaps 10 feet by
12, littered with the inevitable cobwebs, dust, and an
antiquated wooden chair with two legs missing lying on
the left side near the wall. Blade was about to pull away,
when his lamp fell on the rear wall. Or what had once
been the rear wall. Because now a large hole beckoned,
providing access to an adjoining chamber. "This way!"
Blade yelled, and took off, Geronimo dogging his heels.

The Warriors hastened through the opening and discovered another room exactly like the first. But instead
of a dilapidated chair the chamber contained some
newer additions: Private Gatti's blood-soaked helmet
and Dakon II on the floor in the middle of the room.

Blade scooped up the weapon and checked the digital
readout. A full magazine!

"I could use one of those," Geronimo mentioned as
the trio of troopers entered the room.

"Where the hell did you get that?" Captain Wargo

barked, pointing his Dakon II at Blade.

Blade returned the compliment. "It was Gatti's. There's no sign of him."

"Hand it over!" Wargo commanded.

"No way."

Captain Wargo's features contorted into a furious mask. "When I give an order—"

"The Zombies!" Private Kimper interrupted. "Ten yards and closing fast!"

The five men spread out, facing the way they came, their rifles trained on the opening.

Blade looked over his left shoulder. There was a doorway five feet away, lacking a door. Good. They had a way to escape if the Zombies—

Two Zombies rushed into the room, hissing, their arms extended. A barrage of fragmentation bullets ruptured their chests and heads and they collapsed, spewing green fluid.

"Hold them!" Captain Wargo yelled.

Four more Zombies were framed in the opening, and a hail of bullets dropped them on the spot.

Blade frowned. This was easy. Too easy. Almost as if it was a trap. But that would mean the Zombies were behind them—

"Look out!" Geronimo shouted in warning.

Blade crouched and whirled, the Dakon II at hip level, and the movement saved his life. Zombies were pouring in the doorway, and one of them had clawed at the Warrior's neck even as he ducked. Blade let the mutation have it, blowing its face off.

The Technics were firing with total abandon, shooting as quickly as Zombies appeared at the opening or the doorway.

Geronimo, unarmed and feeling utterly helpless, stayed close to Blade.

The Warriors and Technics held their own for a while, downing Zombies until bodies were stacked on both sides of the room.

But then the tide turned.

Blade felt something strike his left shoulder, then his back, and he glanced up at the ceiling in time to see a slavering Zombie plummet through a narrow aperture. "They're above us!" he cried.

Private Kimper was standing three feet from Blade, and he turned to confront this new menace.

Too late.

The Zombie landed between the two men, and with an agility belied by its emaciated appearance, it coiled and pounced, hurtling at Private Kimper, brushing the Technic's Dakon II aside, and fastening its fingers in his throat.

Blade held his fire, concerned he would hit Kimper.

Kimper screamed as he was knocked to the floor, ineffectively flailing at the Zombie with his fists.

Blade closed in and hammered his stock onto the Zombie's head. Once. Twice. Three times, and the Zombie released Kimper and rose, its eyes gleaming savagely. Blade shot it at point-blank range, and his arms and face were pelted with more green gore.

Kimper, gagging, stumbled to his feet and grabbed for his Dakon II.

Three Zombies came through the doorway, and one of them reached Kimper in one mighty bound. The Technic was lifted from his feet and his head was brutally wrenched to the right.

Blade heard the snap of Kimper's vertebra even as he shot the Zombie in the forehead.

Geronimo saw his opportunity. He darted forward and grasped Kimper's Dakon II, then spun, firing, decimating the other two Zombies.

The attack unexpectedly ceased. Dust floated in the air. A preternatural quiet gripped the underground tunnels.

"Blade!" someone gasped.

Blade turned.

Captain Wargo was on his back, a dead Zombie straddling his legs. Four more of the mutations lay near his boots. The Technic was staring at the giant Warrior with a resigned expression, a fatalistic acceptance of his impending demise. "I blew it," he said softly.

Wargo's left arm was gone, missing, severed from his body, no doubt taken by a Zombie intent on consuming the limb as a tasty snack.

"Where's the last commando?" Geronimo asked Blade.

The two Warriors were the only ones standing.

Blade moved to Wargo and knelt next to the officer. He cradled Wargo's head in his left hand, watching the blood pump from the ragged stump where once the left arm had been.

"I've bought it," Wargo stated in a strained whisper.

"We'll get you out of here," Blade told him. "I'll carry you."

Wargo's brow furrowed. "You'd do that for me? After what I've done? After the way I've treated you?"

Blade glanced at the Zombie on Wargo's legs. "We can't let them have you."

Wargo moaned and closed his eyes. When he opened them again, they were rimmed with tears. "I want you to know I was only following orders."

Is that any excuse? Blade wanted to retort. Instead, he smiled and nodded. "I know."

Captain Wargo shuddered. "I'm so cold." He groaned. "I wish . . . I wish. . . ." His head sagged and his eyes shut again.

Geronimo was keeping them covered. "What are we going to do?" he inquired. "Get out of here, I hope."

"We're going after the Genesis Seeds," Blade said.

"But why?" Geronimo rejoined. "You said you doubted they even exist."

"But if they do," Blade explained, "we owe it to our Family, to the entire Civilized Zone, to do our best to retrieve them."

Captain Wargo trembled and coughed, blood appearing at the corners of his mouth. He opened his eyes, which looked haunted. "Don't," he croaked.

Blade leaned closer. "Don't what?"

"Don't go after the seeds." Wargo coughed some more. "They don't exist."

"Then why did your Minister go to so much trouble?" Blade asked. "Why lure us to Technic City and force us to come here? Why?"

"The mind-control gas," Captain Wargo disclosed as

a crimson streak gushed from his right nostril.

Blade and Geronimo exchanged astonished looks.

"The gas was developed by the Institute of Advanced Technology for the Defense Department at the outset of World War Three," Captain Wargo elaborated painfully, wheezing between words. "They planned to use it on the Soviets, but New York was hit before they could transfer the canisters of the gas from here to a military installation." He paused, gathering his breath. "The New York branch wired the Chicago branch of the shipment's readiness minutes before New York was hit. The canisters have been in the underground vault since."

"What does this gas do?" Blade probed.

"Makes a person susceptible to any command they're given," Captain Wargo said. "The Minister . . . intends to make more of it. Use it on the Freedom Federation and the Soviets."

"He wants to conquer the world," Blade observed.

"For the greater glory of the Technics," Wargo stated. "Needs samples to duplicate, like your SEAL."

Blade placed his right hand on Wargo's chest. "The SEAL? What does the SEAL have to do with it?"

Wargo was slipping fast. "Make . . . machines . . . tanks . . . from the same substance . . ."

"Why are you telling us this?" Geronimo asked.

Wargo's eyes fluttered. "Least I could do." His eyes widened, and for a moment he was mentally alert and in full possession of his faculties. He stared at Blade and, unbelievably, laughed, a hard, brittle tittering. "Besides . . . doesn't matter anymore . . . does it?" His body straightened and fluttered, he gasped once, and died.

"I can't say as I'll miss him," Geronimo remarked.

"Me neither," Blade confessed. "But we owe him for telling us about the mind-control gas."

"So what do we do now?" Geronimo questioned.

Blade stood. "We get out of here."

"*Now* you're talking!"

"Go through Kimper's clothes and gear," Blade directed. "We'll need all the spare magazines and ammunition for these Dakon IIs we can find."

"Got you."

The two Warriors searched Wargo and Kimper and found a total of six spare magazines and four boxes of ammunition.

"We'll each take three magazines and two boxes," Blade told Geronimo as he crammed one of the magazines into his right front pocket. He loaded his pockets, then crossed to Private Kimper and crouched next to his body.

"What are you doing?" Geronimo asked.

Blade unfastened the pulse scanner from Kimper's right wrist. "It looks like this gizmo is still on," he said. The screen contained a network of black lines.

"Do you know how to read it?" Geronimo queried hopefully.

"Not really," Blade admitted. "But . . ." He paused. Small, white blips had sprouted on the screen along its outer edge. They were swiftly converging toward the center. "I think company is coming."

"Zombies?"

"Who else?" Blade rose and hurried to the large hole in the wall.

Geronimo followed. "We don't want a canister as a keepsake?"

"The stairs may well be intact on the lower levels," Blade said, "but we're not going to bother finding out. We're going up. And fast."

"I like a man who knows his mind."

They reached the corridor and raced back the way they'd came. Blade saw additional white blips appear on the pulse scanner. If he was reading the thing right, the Zombies were moving toward the room they'd just vacated. And there didn't seem to be any blips corresponding to the hallway they were in. If he was correct, they'd reach the hole allowing access to the level above them without being attacked.

They did.

"How are we going to get up there?" Geronimo asked as his helmet lamp swept the opening 12 feet overhead.

"Easily," Blade said, slinging his Dakon II over his

right shoulder.

"Oh? Are we going to fly?" Geronimo quipped, studying the hole.

"One of us is," Blade responded. Before Geronimo quite knew what had happened, Blade stepped behind his companion, grabbing Geronimo by the back of his belt and the fabric of his green shirt at the nape of his neck.

"Hey! What are you doing?" Geronimo demanded.

"Relax and enjoy the trip," Blade told him. His bulging arms lifted Geronimo and swung his friend down and up, twice in fast succession, gathering speed with each swing. "Get set," he advised.

Geronimo, marveling at Blade's prodigious strength, clasped his Dakon II and grinned.

A third time Blade swung his fellow Warrior, and then he heaved and released his grip.

Geronimo was propelled through the opening, landing on his stomach with his legs suspended from the hole. He used his elbows to crawl to his feet, then looked down at Blade. "And how are you going to make it?"

Blade gauged the distance. "It's too high to jump."

"You'd best hurry," Geronimo cautioned him.

Blade glanced at the pulse scanner. "I agree." White blips were moving his way. He unslung the Dakon II.

"I've got an idea," Geronimo said.

"Make it fast," Blade stated. The blips were much closer.

Geronimo placed his Dakon II on the floor and removed his shirt. "Here!" He held onto one sleeve and dropped the shirt through the hole.

Blade scanned the corridor behind him, then looked at the shirt. The other sleeve was dangling about nine feet over his head. An easy jump for one of his enormous stature.

Footsteps pounded in the hallway to his rear.

Blade whirled, his helmet light illuminating four hissing Zombies closing in, four more of the detestable deviates with a craving for healthy human flesh. Blade blasted them with the Dakon.

The Zombies danced spasmodically as they were struck, then fell.

More blips filled the pulse scanner. Blade reslung the Dakon, crouched, and leaped, his arms stretched to their limit, his fingers clamping on the shirt and holding fast. "Pull!"

Geronimo was nearly upended. The weight was almost too much for his arms to bear. Crouched at the rim, he sagged, about to pitch forward, but caught himself in the nick of time. He gritted his teeth as his arms strained to raise Blade a couple of feet, hoping the shirt would hold. The Family Weavers had constructed his clothing, and their garments were renowned for their durability. But Blade felt as if he weighed a ton!

"Hurry!" Blade prompted him.

Every muscle on Geronimo's stocky body quivered as he rose an inch, then several more.

Swaying below the hole, Blade waited, his body taut. If Geronimo could get him close enough to the rim . . .

Something suddenly encircled the Warrior's legs.

Blade looked down, dumbfounded to see a Zombie clinging to his ankles. The creature's teeth were exposed as it snarled and snapped at his leg, tearing into his fatigue pants but missing the skin underneath.

Geronimo felt the shirt wrench to one side, and he glanced down.

Blade twisted, striving to extricate his legs, hoping the Zombie would not succeed in taking a chunk out of him. An insane idea occurred to him, a desperate maneuver to disentangle his legs and reach the level above. He balled his right fist and lashed downward, his left hand bearing the brunt of his massive weight, and crashed his fist into the Zombie's hairless skull.

Staggered by the blow, the Zombie released its grip and glared up at its dinner.

Which was exactly what Blade wanted.

The giant Warrior drew his legs up to his chest, then lashed his feet down, deliberately driving his boots onto the Zombie's slim shoulders. In the instant his soles made contact, Blade pushed upward, using the Zombie as a springboard, uncoiling and springing through the hole in the floor to sprawl beside Geronimo.

Geronimo tumbled backwards, landing on his posterior. He yanked on his shirt and smiled at Blade. "What? No full gainer?"

"Let's go!" Blade said, rising.

Geronimo hastily donned his shirt, and they fled, retracing their route, following the trail of their footprints in the dust. They arrived at the door leading to the stairs and paused, breathing heavily, leaning on the walls.

"Didn't we leave this door open?" Geronimo asked.

Blade couldn't recall. He shrugged and tugged on the door, grateful it flew open so readily.

Until he saw what lurked on the other side.

The landing was jammed with Zombies and the stairs were packed with more.

"They were waiting for us!" Geronimo cried.

Blade leveled the Dakon II as the front row started toward them. They were overwhelmingly outnumbered, and outrunning the monstrosities would be impossible at this close range. He could only hope to sell his life dearly, and he would have done so had not a very peculiar event transpired.

One of the Zombies uttered a weird, gurgling noise, and the effect on the assembled mutations was instantaneous and bewildering. They abruptly ran off, the majority heading up the stairs in a confused panic, while a dozen or so bolted past a startled pair of Warriors flattened against the corridor walls.

"What was that all about?" Geronimo nervously inquired after the last Zombie was lost to view.

"Beats me," Blade said. "But whatever it was, I like it! Let's get to the SEAL."

They walked through the doorway to the landing.

Geronimo bent his neck, craning skyward. "I can see the top!" he exclaimed. "And there isn't a Zombie in sight!"

"Good riddance," Blade commented. Now nothing would stop them.

Or so he thought.

There was a rumbling roar from directly below, and

the very tunnel shook, the stairs vibrating and the landing the Warriors occupied shimmying.

Blade, nearest the railing, leaned over the edge for an unobstructed view of the vertical shaft. The . . . thing . . . his helmet lamp revealed caused the short hairs on the back of his neck to rise, his skin tingling, and he unconsciously stepped away from the railing, staggered.

"What is it?" Geronimo asked, moving toward the railing.

Blade grabbed his friend by the shoulder and shoved, sending Geronimo in the direction of the steps. "Go!" he shouted, forgetting Geronimo could hear the slightest sound in his helmet earphone.

"But . . ." Geronimo protested, his left foot on the bottom step.

"*Go*!" Blade yelled.

Geronimo, disturbed and alarmed, took the stairs two at a bound. "Come on!" he urged Blade.

But Blade had other ideas. He would delay the . . . thing . . . until Geronimo reached safety. It was the only way one of them would get out alive. He stepped to the railing and gazed downward.

Just as the thing gave another deafening roar and rushed toward the landing.

16

"Turn in there," Hickok directed.

Spencer immediately complied, pulling the four-wheeler into a parking lot.

Hickok scanned the lot, noting a lot of civilians and trikes and other vehicles, but the Technic police weren't in evidence.

Good.

"Pull into that parking space," Hickok instructed the Technic.

Spencer parked between two other four-wheelers, one of them red, the other brown like his. "What now?"

"We sit here," Hickok said. He needed time to think. They were about three miles from the Central Core. Dozens of Technic police and military vehicles had passed them along the way, but the security forces were all headed toward the Core. Most likely, the Technics believed he was still in the vicinity of the Core. And they undoubtedly had their hands full cleaning up the mess he'd created with the truck. Not to mention the reaction the Minister's death would create, the turmoil it would stir up.

"How long?" Spencer inquired.

Hickok glared. "Until I say otherwise. Got it?"

"Yes, sir," Spencer said feebly.

"Turn the other way," Hickok instructed him. "Count the trikes for a spell."

Spencer twisted, his back to the gunfighter.

Hickok quickly reloaded the giant cartridges in his

right Python, keeping the revolver out of sight between his knees. As he was slipping the last cartridge into the cylinder, he suddenly realized something was missing. He'd forgotten Blade's Commando! He'd left it on the floor of the truck! "Damnit!" he declared in annoyance.

Spencer turned in his seat. "What did I do?" he asked in a fright.

"Nothin', idiot!" Hickok said. "Turn around or else!"

Spencer obeyed.

Hickok sighed, pondering his next move. He had to bust out of Technic City. The question was *how*? How to get past a mine field and an electrified fence with enough juice to fry him to a cinder? How to elude the scores of Technic police and military types on his tail? And how to reach the safety of the Home, alone and on foot? This wasn't turning out to be a piece of cake after all.

What to do?

Hickok idly surveyed the buildings surrounding the parking lot on three sides. One of them, a two-story structure with pastel walls, supported a billboard on the side visible from the lot. A beautiful woman was seated at an elegant restaurant, a bowl of soup on the table in front of her, a heaping spoonful close to her red lips.

A siren wailed in the distance.

Hickok absently read the billboard as he deliberated.

"THE FINEST DINING IN TECHNIC CITY! AT A PRICE YOU CAN AFFORD! KURTZ'S ON THE MALL, AT 64TH AND THE DIAGONAL! SHRIMP . . . $125. STEWED WORMS . . . $90. WORMS A LA KING . . . $110. A DELECTABLE TREAT FOR THE TASTE BUDS! RESERVATIONS ARE—"

Worms?

Hickok's mind belatedly registered the menu advertised. He read it again.

Worms?

"What's that mean?" Hickok demanded.

"What's what mean?" Spencer responded, watching

the traffic.

"That!" Hickok declared, pointing at the billboard.

"Can I turn around now?" Spencer wanted to know.

"Turn around!" Hickok stated, still pointing. "And tell me what that is all about."

Spencer shifted and gazed at the billboard. After a moment he looked at the gunman. "You've never seen a billboard before? Where are you from?"

"I'm talking about what's on the billboard," Hickok said, correcting the Technic.

Spencer seemed puzzled. "It's called an advertisement."

"I figured that out for myself," Hickok declared archly. "I want to know about the food."

"Oh," Spencer said, as if that explained everything. "Well, shrimp is a seafood. We get ours from the Androixians—"

"I know what the blazes seafood is!" Hickok cut Spencer short. "What about the worms?"

"Worms are these creepy-crawling things which live in the ground," Spencer explained. "They—"

Hickok's flinty blue eyes had narrowed. "Are you doin' this on purpose?"

"Doing what on purpose?"

"I know what worms are," Hickok said, peeved. "Why are they on the menu?"

"I'm not certain I follow you," Spencer said. "Worms are on the menu at every restaurant and diner in Technic City."

Hickok was shocked. "You mean to tell me you folks eat worms?"

"Do you mean to tell me you don't?" Spencer replied.

"But worms! How can you eat worms?" Hickok asked, nauseated by the mere idea.

"Worms are quite tasty," Spencer said. "You should try them sometime."

Hickok grimaced. "Not on your life."

"Everybody eats worms," Spencer detailed.

"Not where I come from," Hickok said. "I've never heard of anybody eatin' worms. What a bunch of cow chips!"

"What kind of food do you eat?" Spencer asked.

"Our Tillers grow a heap of vegetables," Hickok said, "and we have some fruit, but our meat is usually venison."

"What's venison?"

Hickok squinted at the Technic. "You're puttin' me on."

"We don't have venison," Spencer said. "What is it?"

"Deer meat."

"What's a deer?"

"You've never seen a deer?" Hickok queried incredulously.

"No. Is it some kind of animal? Animals are illegal in Technic City," Spencer disclosed.

"What about dogs and cats?"

"They're popular," Spencer commented, "but, personally, I don't like them as much as worms."

"You eat dogs and cats?" Hickok questioned him.

"You don't?"

Hickok studied the billboard, perplexed. He could understand eating dogs, because feral dogs were a rare Family fare. But worms! Revolting! He gazed around the parking lot, stared at the crowded avenue beyond, and perceived a spark of sanity in the notion. Technic City contained millions of people, all fenced in like cattle, herded into a limited area and forced to live out their manipulated lives subject to every whim of the totalitarian regime controlling them. With so many mouths to feed, and with scant dietary resources, the Technics had supplanted the typical prewar fare with the one food source capable of breeding faster than rabbits; with an abundant animal readily available at any time of year; with a creature easily cultivated and processed: worms. When you looked at it logically, Hickok grudgingly admitted, the idea sort of made sense.

Another siren sounded from afar.

Hickok dismissed the worms from his mind and concentrated on his escape. He glanced at Spencer. "I want you to tell me everything you know about this buggy of yours.''

"Everything?"

"Everything," Hickok affirmed. "How it runs, how you stop it, what those things are on the ends of the handlebars I saw you turning. Everything."

Spencer commenced his instruction, and as the gunman listened, fascinated, a crafty scheme blossomed, a devious ploy designed to achieve his deliverance from the vile metropolis of worm-eaters.

17

The . . . thing . . . scrambled up the tunnel wall toward the landing, snarling viciously.

Blade had seen more than his share of genetically deformed mutations over the years. There had been mutates galore, and the Brutes in Thief River Falls, and Fant in the Twin Cities, and the Doktor's bizarre creatures such as Lynx, Gremlin, and Ferret. But never had he witnessed anything as horrendous as the mutant in the shaft.

The beast was an amalgam of insect-like traits. Its huge body resembled that of a centipede, with five over-sized segments and two legs on each segment. The body and legs were black, and the legs ended in tapered claws. Its head appeared fly-like, but it had four eyes, all bright green, instead of the usual two. Its elongated jaws were like those of a praying mantis, but glistening between the jaws were two rows of pointed, spiderish fangs.

Blade took all of this in as he rested the Dakon barrel on the metal railing and crouched, aiming for the creature's bloated cranium. He remembered the button on the scope and pressed it to activate the Laser Sighting Mode, and there it was, a bright red dot on the creature's sloping forehead.

The mutant was 15 feet below the landing, its claws clinging to the sheer walls, finding purchase where any other animal would slip to its doom.

Blade squeezed the trigger, the Dakon II recoiling

into his shoulder.

The creature rocked as its forehead exploded, spraying the wall with black flesh, a pale yellowish muck oozing from the cavity, but it kept coming, climbing higher.

The mutant was only ten feet from the landing now.

Blade frowned, perturbed. He'd gone for the head, for the brain, hoping to dispatch the thing with a minimum of fuss. His shots should have struck the brain, killing it.

If it had a brain.

He aimed again and fired.

The creature shrieked as its squat neck was hit, its jaws twitching.

But it kept coming.

Seven feet now.

Blade rose and pressed the trigger, sweeping the Dakon in an arc.

The fragmentation bullets stitched a straight line across the mutant's segmented body, geysers of flesh and pulpy gore raining on the wall.

But it kept coming.

And there wasn't time for another broadside.

Blade retreated toward the stairs, watching the landing edge for the first sign of the mutant. There was a loud scraping noise in his amplified right earphone, emanating from underneath the landing.

Directly underneath.

Blade paused. But that would mean the thing was crawling under the landing to the other side, using the landing as a shield from the Dakon.

That would mean he was being outflanked!

Blade spun, finding his deduction was accurate.

The mutant had passed under the landing and climbed up the railing behind its prey. It was perched on the railing, its head swaying as it examined its next meal.

Blade raised the Dakon.

Snarling, the creature flowed over the top rail, its head and first two segments reaching the landing in a blurred streak. It reared on its lower segments, then pounced like a bird taking a fish, its serrated jaws spearing down and in.

Blade was caught before he could react. He felt something strike both sides of the helmet, and the mutant's first pair of legs reached up, its claws digging into his broad shoulders.

It had him!

Blade rammed the Dakon barrel into the creature's exposed abdomen and blasted away.

The mutant wrenched its iron jaws upward, tearing the strapless helmet from the Warrior's head. It screeched as its jaws closed, crushing the helmet as effortlessly as a man would break an eggshell. Enraged by the agony in its belly, it flung its prey across the landing and into the opposite railing.

Blade's left side bore the brunt of the impact, and he doubled over as an excruciating spasm lanced his chest. The Dakon II dropped from his benumbed fingers, and he fell to his knees, gasping for air. He saw the creature climb the rest of the way over the railing.

The mutant's ghastly head and the first two segments of its hideous body rose from the floor, like a snake about to strike. It silently rocked from side to side, its jaws slowly opening and closing, opening and closing.

The squashed helmet was on the landing to its left.

If only he had his Bowies! He could dive under the monster and slash its guts out with a few swift swipes. But he didn't have them, and Blade sensed he might never see them again if he didn't come up with something fast. What he needed the most was a diversion, a distraction.

And he got it.

A loud war whoop from the stairs above caused the creature to bend its neck straight up as it searched for the source of the cry.

Geronimo was between landings, leaning over the railing. He aimed at the four green eyes and fired, sweeping the Dakon from side to side.

The mutant howled and thrashed, its head tilted, attempting to avoid the rain of lead. It suddenly bellowed and turned, its front sections climbing into the railing as it started up after this new pest.

Blade saw his chance. He rose, the Dakon II in his left hand, and ran toward the creature, grabbing the pulverized helmet as he did.

The monster's head and first section stretched toward Geronimo, momentarily suspended in midair.

Blade pointed the Dakon at the mutant's jaw below the head and squeezed the trigger.

The creature's throat erupted in a shower of black flesh and pale ooze, and it whipped its head down, jaws wide, primed to rip its quarry to shreds.

Blade swung the ruined helmet around and up, driving it into the thing's mouth, into its fangs, and as the mutant instinctively snapped its jaws shut, he released the helmet and stepped back, lowering the Dakon and firing at the mutant's body segments, at the top of its legs, at the joints, where the legs were attached to the individual segments, and the fragmentation bullets did as he wanted, rupturing the limbs, bursting the joints, blowing four of the creature's legs from its body.

With only four sets of claws still gripping the railing, the thing started to slip, loosing its balance, lurching precariously on the brink of the precipice.

Blade decided to help it along. He ran up to the mutant, reversing his hold on the Dakon II, gripping it by the barrel, and as the creature struggled to right itself, its grotesque head swinging down to the landing as its pair of front legs clawed for a purchase, he whipped the rifle like a club, slamming the stock into the monster's face.

The thing snarled and swiped its jaws at the Warrior's head.

Blade ducked and came up swinging, the butt end of the gun digging into the mutant's left eyes.

Furious, the creature lunged at its foe.

Blade dodged, then rammed the Dakon's barrel into the mutant's eyes, shifted his hands, and squeezed the trigger.

The thing was staggered. It reared up, in extreme torment, forgetting four of its legs were gone.

Blade closed in, firing, the fragmentation bullets exploding two more limbs from the hideous segments.

Incensed beyond measure, the mutant tried to turn and crush its adversary. The motion was more than its remaining legs could tolerate. It lost its footing and pitched over the railing, uttering a shrill scream as it plummeted into the inky gloom below.

Blade grasped the railing and leaned forward, listening, waiting for the creature to hit bottom. Or would it? Maybe the monster would arrest its fall by catching hold of a jutting pipe or beam. Maybe it would attack him again before he could reach the surface! He held his breath, tuned to his right ear amplifier.

The mutant's scream decreased in volume as it dropped, and its death cry was punctuated by a dull thud coming from the very bottom of the shaft. Then all was quiet.

Blade waited with baited breath, straining to detect a noise, to learn if the creature was going to renew its assault.

"Are you coming, or are you admiring the view?"

Blade glanced up at Geronimo. "On my way," he said, and ran up the stairs.

"Let's get out of here!" Geronimo stated as Blade rejoined him.

"You get no argument from me," Blade said.

Side by side, the Warriors hurriedly ascended the shaft to the tunnel entrance. They stopped on the rim and glanced down.

"What are we going to do about these canisters containing the mind-control gas?" Geronimo asked. "If we leave them there, the Technics will eventually find a way of retrieving them."

"I know," Blade said thoughtfully. "We can't let that happen."

"So what do we do?"

Blade studied the abandoned jeeps and trucks. "You check the jeeps. I'll check the trucks."

"What am I looking for?" Geronimo inquired.

"See if they have any gas left in them," Blade said.

"And look for spare gas cans or anything else we can use."

A quick search confirmed a minimum of half a tank of gas in each vehicle, and they discovered four spare gas cans in one of the trucks.

"This will do," Blade declared as he opened one of the cans.

"For what?" Geronimo queried.

"Find a hose we can use to siphon the gas from them," Blade directed.

Geronimo removed a hose from a jeep engine to serve as the siphon. "What now?"

Blade attended to the task of siphoning the gas, filling all four gas cans.

"I still don't get it," Geronimo said as Blade filled the last.

"Take two of these cans," Blade told him. "Pour the gas over the three jeeps. I'll do the same to the four trucks. Hurry, before the Zombies come after us."

Within minutes, all seven Technic vehicles were reeking from the pungent stench of the gasoline.

"Now what?" Geronimo asked.

"Refill the gas cans," Blade ordered. He covered Geronimo while more gas was siphoned from the jeeps and trucks.

"All done," Geronimo announced.

"Look in the trucks," Blade said. "I saw some rags in one of them. Find four rags we can use."

Geronimo, deducing Blade's plan, jogged to the trucks and collected the rags.

"Okay. Stick the rags into the top of the gas cans," Blade instructed. "Leave about six inches protruding from the can."

"Enough to light with a match," Geronimo commented.

"You got it." Blade ran to the SEAL, unlocked the driver's door, and climbed in. The transport purred to life as soon as he turned the key. He slowly drove toward the nearest jeep, aligning the SEAL's grill with the jeep's rear bumper. He'd never tried this before, and he wasn't positive it would work. Gingerly, he slowly accelerated, the SEAL's powerful engine surging as the transport pressed against the jeep. Blade increased his pressure on the accelerator, confident the immense transport could achieve his goal.

"Hold it!" Geronimo suddenly shouted. He ran up to the SEAL. "I just noticed! They left the key in the ignition! Probably wanted to be ready for a quick getaway! I'll put it in neutral!"

"Go for it!" Blade stated.

Geronimo slid into the jeep and twisted the key. The motor refused to kick over, but he found he could work the gearshift if he positioned the key halfway between Off and On. He shifted the jeep into neutral and jumped out.

Blade eased the SEAL forward, and this time the jeep was easily propelled forward, toward the shaft, up to the rim and over the rim, a rolling, metallic din echoing from the tunnel as the jeep tumbled and crashed to the bottom of the shaft.

Geronimo smiled and held his right thumb up.

Working rapidly, the two Warriors pushed one vehicle after the other into the tunnel. One of the trucks caught on the lip and had to be angled to the side before it plunged over the edge. Finally, the job was done.

Blade leaped to the ground and joined Geronimo at the shaft rim. "Here," he said, holding up the box of waterproof matches he'd taken from the SEAL's glove compartment, a new box recently received in trade from the Civilized Zone.

Geronimo lined up the four gas cans next to the tunnel.

Blade knelt and removed a match from the box. "Ready?"

"Ready as I'll ever be," Geronimo responded.

Blade quickly lit each rag, and only after all four were ablaze did he hand the matches to Geronimo. "This is for Hickok," he stated grimly, and with two swift flicks of his right foot he knocked all four cans into the shaft. "Move!"

They sprinted to the SEAL and clambered inside.

Blade gunned the engine and wheeled the transport in a right circle, heading for the Hudson, gaining speed. Ten. Twenty. Forty. And they were fifty yards from the tunnel when it blew, a fiery column of red and orange billowing skyward from the shaft, as an enormous explosion rocked the underground network.

Geronimo, looking over his right shoulder, whistled. "You should see it! The flames must be two hundred feet in the air!"

"So much for the mind-control gas," Blade said.

"What did you mean back there?" Geronimo probed. "About Hickok?"

"I doubt the Minister would keep him alive," Blade declared angrily.

"You don't think so? But what about the hostage we're holding at the Home? Farrow?"

"So what?" Blade retorted. "Do you really believe the Minister gives a damn about any of his people?"

"No," Geronimo admitted morosely.

"If the Minister hasn't killed Hickok yet," Blade said, "he will when we don't show up as expected. We can't go back there alone."

"What will we do?" Geronimo asked.

"We'll go back the same way we came," Blade stated. "We'll bypass Technic City." His fists clenched on the steering wheel. "And when we reach the Home, we'll call a Freedom Federation Council and urge them to declare war on the Technics."

"And what if they won't go along with us?"

"Then we'll do it alone," Blade vowed.

"The Family against the Technics? Won't we be a bit outnumbered?" Geronimo queried.

"We'll do it ourselves!" Blade promised vehemently. "We'll make them pay for their deceit! Their treachery must not go unpunished!" He glanced at Geronimo. "Besides, Hickok would want us to avenge him."

Geronimo shook his head. "I agree with you, but I can't accept the idea of Hickok being dead."

"Why not?"

"I don't know. It's hard to define. But Hickok has more dumb luck than any ten people I know. If there's a

way out of Technic City," Geronimo predicted,
"Hickok will find it."

"I don't see how."

18

The guard stationed at tower number four on the west side of Technic City turned to his three companions. "Who brought the cards?"

"We'd best hold off," one of the other soldiers said.

"Why?" the first one rejoined. "The captain made his rounds an hour ago. It's almost midnight. No one is going to bother us this late at night."

"I know," the other agreed. "But we're still on alert. They haven't found that Warrior yet, and they might conduct a surprise inspection."

"Yeah," chimed in a third trooper. "We'd better wait."

The first guard sighed. "Okay. Whatever you guys want. But I think you're making a mistake. You know how boring third shift can be."

"Better safe than sorry," opined the second soldier.

The first man shrugged and stared at the darkened city to the east. Curfew was at ten, and lights out in individual domiciles was set at eleven. Public buildings could stay lit until midnight. He could see the Central Core on the horizon, brilliantly illuminated by hundreds of lights, the heart of the city, a beacon in the night. He reflected on the day's news: the escape of the Warrior known as Hickok from the Core. He marveled at the Warrior's ingenuity. No one had ever busted out of the Central Core before. And he ruminated on the rumors spreading like wildfire through the city, rumors asserting the Minister and his First Secretary were dead.

The paper, radio, and tube hadn't mentioned the deaths, and the guard doubted they were true. He knew how readily gossip could circulate.

A sharp noise reached the tower, coming from the surrounding darkness, from the vicinity of the mine field.

"Did you hear something?" the first guard asked.

"Nothing," the second responded.

"You're hearing things," said the third.

"Probably," the first trooper grudgingly conceded. He gazed at the mine field, deliberately blackened to complicate escape attempts. Anyone would think twice before venturing across a mine field at night, never knowing when they might accidentally tread on a mine and be obliterated by a gigantic explosion.

Another sound became audible, the muted rumbling of a motor.

"Do you hear it now?" the first guard demanded. He was young and wanted to impress the others with his superior senses.

"Sounds like a trike," remarked one of the others.

"But who would be out with a trike at this time of night?" queried the young trooper. "The captain would be in his jeep."

They moved to the east side of the tower, listening. The trike motor abruptly revved louder.

"It must be the Warrior!" the second soldier exclaimed. "He's going to try and break through the gate!"

A beam of light abruptly appeared on the far side of the mine field.

"Here he comes!" cried the second soldier.

"No he's not!" disputed the third. "Look! He's going to try and make it across the mine field!"

Sure enough, the light zoomed toward the mine field, streaking for the far side.

"The fool will never make it," said the young trooper.

The trike was bobbing and bouncing as it raced across the field. It swerved from side to side in a weaving pattern.

"He'll never make it," reiterated the young guard, cradling his Dakon II in his arms.

A sparkling blast rent the air as the trike struck one of the mines. A ball of flame and smoke coalesced for several seconds, then dispersed.

"What a jerk," the young trooper said.

"You stay here," directed the second soldier. "We'll take the flashlights and the mine map and go have a look. Call HQ and tell them what happened."

"Right away," the youthful guard replied.

The young guard walked to the Communications Console while his three friends hastened down the tower steps. He picked up the headset and pressed the appropriate buttons. "Private Casey here," he said when the sergeant at the ComCenter in the Central Core answered. "Inform Captain Zorn we have a Priority Two. Repeat. Priority Two." He listened for a moment. "Yes, sir. On their way now." He glanced at his watch. "ETA five minutes? Yes, sir. Over and out." He replaced the headset and walked to the east side of the tower, watching through the window as his three companions moved across the field toward the smoldering wreckage of the trike. Their flashlights were proceeding very slowly, as they cautiously advanced while consulting the minefield map to insure they didn't step on a mine and wind up the way the driver of the trike had.

"Freeze!"

Private Casey tensed at the barked command. He started to turn his head.

"I said freeze!" the harsh voice warned. "One more twitch and you'll be feedin' the worms instead of vice versa!"

"Who are you? What do you want?" Casey asked.

"I'll do the talkin', pipsqueak! Set your piece on the floor, real easy like!"

Private Casey hesitated. He knew his duty. He should whirl and confront this stranger. But there was something about the man's deep voice, a steely vibrancy, a "Don't mess with me or else!" quality he found unnerving. He intuitively sensed he would die instantly if he disobeyed this man, and Casey didn't want to die. He laid the Dakon II on the floor.

"That's real sensible for a Technic," the stranger said.

Casey waited, expecting to hear the man cross the tower. Instead, something hard was jammed into his spine.

"Turn around!" the voice commanded.

Private Casey complied, discovering a lean blond man in buckskins with a rifle over each shoulder, a revolver under his left arm, and two more revolvers, both pearl-handled silver jobs, in his hands.

"Where's the key to the gate?" the blond man demanded.

"I can't give it to you," Casey mustered the courge to say.

The gunman sighed. "I'm tired, pipsqueak. Real tired. And I don't have the time to play games." He cocked the right revolver. "If you don't tell me where they keep the key to the gate, I'm gonna shoot you in the nuts."

Casey swallowed, and a prickly sensation erupted over his balls.

"I ain't got all night!" the gunman snapped.

Casey pointed at a desk in the northwest corner. "It's in the top drawer on the right."

"Thanks." The gunman sidled to the desk and opened the drawer.

"You're Hickok, aren't you?" Casey asked.

The gunman nodded as he withdrew a large key on a metal ring.

"I knew it!" Casey said. He didn't know what to do or say, and he was too excited to remain silent. "Did you really kill the Minister?" he blurted.

"Yep."

"I can't believe it!" Casey exclaimed, awed.

"How do I turn off the fence?" Hickok inquired.

"There's a circuit breaker in a box to the left of the gate," Casey revealed.

"What's a circuit breaker?" Hickok responded.

"Look for an orange lever," Casey said. "Pull it

down and you'll turn off the current."

Hickok moved to the window and watched the trio of guards heading for the flaming debris in the mine field.

"Who was on the trike?" Casey asked.

"Nobody," Hickok answered.

"But trikes don't run by themselves," Casey stated.

"They do if you help 'em along a little," Hickok said. He motioned toward the stairs. "Let's go. You first."

Private Casey led off. "Are . . . are you going to kill me?"

"I'm not in the habit of gunnin' pipsqueaks," Hickok declared. "But don't push me or I might make an exception in your case."

They reached the steps to the ground. "How did you do it?" Casey queried as he descended.

"Wasn't too hard," Hickok said. "A bozo by the name of Spencer told me how the trikes run. To pick up speed, you have to turn a thingumajig on the handlebars. And to shift, your foot presses on a thingamabob. Hope I'm not bein' too technical for you."

"I know how to drive a trike," Casey told him.

"Then you'll appreciate how I did it," Hickok remarked. "I fired her up, with the shift in neutral, and turned the accelerator to where I wanted it. Then I tied it in place with Spencer's shoelaces. Those grips have deep ridges in 'em, so it was real easy to keep it from slippin' too much. After that, I kicked the buggy into gear and—presto!—the decoy I needed."

"Pretty clever," Private Casey admitted.

Hickok sighed. "Where's Geronimo when I need him?"

"Geronimo?" Casey said, puzzled.

"A pard of mine," Hickok stated. "Believe it or not, I don't get complimented on my smarts too much. I wish he'd been here to hear it."

"Wasn't one of the other Warriors captured with you named Geronimo?" Casey asked.

Hickok stopped. "Yeah. Have you heard anything about him or my other buddy, Blade?"

"You know they went to New York City?"

"So I was told."

Private Casey shifted uneasily. "I don't know how to tell you this." He stared at the pearl-handled revolvers.

"Give it to me straight," Hickok directed.

"It's not official," Casey said anxiously.

"Spill the beans!" Hickok ordered.

"We lost contact with them," Casey disclosed. "Now remember," he quickly added, "it's just some scuttlebutt I picked up. It hasn't been confirmed."

Hickok's features were obscured by the shadows. They were standing near the fence, the gate illumined by a spotlight on top of the guard tower. "Turn off the current," he said gruffly.

"I thought you were going to do it," Casey said.

"I can't. You see, I've got me this new motto I live by," the gunman declared.

"New motto?"

"Never, ever trust a lyin' skunk of a Technic!" Hickok stated harshly.

Private Casey gulped.

"Now kill the blasted fence!" Hickok commanded.

Casey immediately complied.

"Now the gate." Hickok tossed the key to the trooper.

Private Casey unlocked the gate and shoved it open.

Hickok strode up to the soldier and glared at him, nose to nose. "You've got two ways of playin' this, pipsqueak. You can run upstairs after I leave, and blab what happened to the bigwigs. Or you can play it safe and keep your mouth shut. It's up to you."

"If I report this, I'll be court-martialed," Casey predicted. "I'll wind up in prison or in front of a firing squad."

"So keep your big mouth closed," Hickok advised. "No one will ever know I was here except for us. They'll all reckon I was blown sky-high in the mine field. I left the varmint who owned the trike tied up back at a worm farm. He'll get loose soon and tell the authorities I stole it from him. They'll put two and two together."

"I really am going to live!" Private Casey exclaimed.

"I told you I wouldn't kill you."

"But they said you're a cold-blooded murderer," Casey remarked.

"A lot of folks think that way," Hickok conceded. He thought of the boy lying in the pool of blood. "But they don't know about my other new motto. Never, ever kill unless it's absolutely necessary."

"I like that motto," Casey remarked.

Hickok grinned. "You're all right, pipsqueak." He started through the gate, then paused. "Say, will they know you cut the juice to the fence?"

Private Casey nodded. "It'll register on the monitor in the Central Core."

"If they ask, tell 'em you don't know a thing," Hickok suggested.

"Lie?"

"Can you come up with a better way to save your hide?" Hickok asked.

Casey considered for a moment. "Nope."

"Then as soon as I skedaddle, close the gate and open the circuit. They might believe it was a temporary short."

"All of a sudden you're not as dumb as you act," Casey said.

"Thanks. I think." Hickok walked through the gate, holstered his left Python, and waved. "As a pard of mine might say, may the Great Spirit bless all your endeavors."

The night swallowed the gunman.

Private Casey blinked a few times, wondering if the incident might have been a dream. The killer of the Minister had spared his life! He hastily closed the gate, reset the circuit breaker, and ran up the stairs to the tower. The red light above the headset was blinking. He scooped it up and cleared his throat.

"Private Casey here . . . Sorry, sir, I was watching the mine field. . . . Yes, they're almost to the point. . . . No, the captain hasn't arrived yet. . . . Turned off the fence? No, sir. Why would I do that? . . . No, sir, I didn't notice. I was watching the mine field. . . . Yes, sir, those damn transformers can be a pain in the ass. . . . Of course, sir."

Casey replaced the headset, beaming. He'd done it! Now there was just one thing he wanted to know: what the hell was the Great Spirit?

19

Everything was proceeding according to the Minister's plan! The Home would soon be history!

Lieutenant Alicia Farrow smiled, her white teeth a sharp contrast to the inky night. Her luminous watch indicated the time was 15 minutes past midnight. In another 15 minutes the demolition team would come over the west wall, and she must be there to greet them. She had crept from B Block 10 minutes ago, and now was poised at the foot of the stairs leading from the inner bank of the moat to the rampart. The wooden stairs were located a few feet south of the closed drawbridge. She cautiously climbed the steps, scanning the rampart, searching for the Warrior on duty. She knew Omega Triad was scheduled, and she expected to find Ares manning the west wall as was his custom.

A dark form moved to her right, directly over the drawbridge.

Farrow squinted. It was a Warrior, patrolling the rampart. But something was wrong. The figure wasn't tall enough to be Ares. It was definitely a man, which ruled out Helen. And it lacked a hat, eliminating Sundance because he always wore a black sombrero.

So who the hell was it?

Farrow reached the top of the stairs and stopped, perplexed. The figure was gone! One instant it had been there, the next it had vanished! Had whoever it was seen her? Was he—

"Hello, Alicia."

Farrow gripped the rail to keep from plunging into the moat. Her senses were swimming. Not him! It couldn't be him!

But it was.

Yama materialized beside her, his Wilkinson in his right hand. "I'm surprised to see you here," he said softly. "You haven't spoken a word to me all day."

Farrow tried to speak but couldn't. Her mouth refused to respond.

"What did I do to upset you?" Yama asked.

"What are *you* doing here?" Farrow exclaimed.

"I have the night shift," Yama responded.

"But Ares is supposed to be here," Farrow asserted. "Omega Triad has wall duty tonight."

"I know," Yama said. "But Ares isn't feeling too well. The Review Board cleared him, but he's still upset. He's been moping around B Block since it happened. I offered to fill in for him tonight."

"Oh no!" Farrow said.

Yama moved closer. "What's wrong? Did you want to see Ares?"

"No," Farrow replied. "I expected him to be here, is all."

"I don't understand," Yama stated. "You didn't want to see Ares, but you expected him to be here?"

"Yeah," Farrow said nervously. "I wanted some fresh air, so I climbed up here. I knew Ares was on duty, but I didn't want to run into him. See?"

"Hmmmm," was all Yama said.

Now what was she going to do? Farrow knew the demolition team would arrive at any minute. And the first thing they would do after scaling the wall would be to snuff Yama. Yama! He was a lowlife, but she still felt affection for him. The prospect of his death was profoundly upsetting.

"If you'd rather be alone, I'll leave," Yama offered.

"No!" Farrow blurted out. She frantically racked her brain for a solution. If she could get him off the wall! "Care to walk along the moat with me?"

"You know I can't leave my post," Yama said.

Farrow saw him look from side to side, then stare at her. She squirmed uncomfortably, emotionally distraught.

"Stay here," Yama directed. He turned and moved to the middle of the rampart.

What was he doing?

"What are you doing?"

Yama didn't answer. She heard a scratching sound, and a lantern abruptly lit up the central section of the rampart. Yama was next to the lantern, blowing on a match.

Farrow hurried over to the Warrior. "Why'd you do that?"

The lantern was suspended from an iron hook imbedded in the lip of the rampart, just below the strands of barbed wire encircling the entire walled compound. Its flickering light played over his silver hair and mustache as he slowly turned to face her. His blue eyes bored into her. "I wanted to see you clearly," he said.

"But isn't it dangerous," she protested, "having the lantern on this way? Anyone out there," and she waved at the surrounding forest, "could see you."

Yama shrugged. "I doubt anyone is out there. Few people would be abroad in the woods at night. It's too hazardous."

Farrow fidgeted, repeatedly glancing at the tree line.

"Is something wrong?" Yama asked.

"I'm fine!" Farrow responded, her tone edgy.

"Come with me," Yama said. He took her by the left forearm and led her to the left, away from the lantern, to the stairs. He stopped on the upper step, both of them now shrouded in semi-darkness.

"What are you doing?" Farrow inquired.

"We're going to stand here for a while and enjoy the night sky," Yama told her.

Farrow tried to pull her arm free. "I'd like to go."

"I'd imagine you would," Yama said, his right hand a vise on her arm.

"You're hurting me!" Farrow objected.

Yama's right hand clamped tighter. "And how many innocent Family members did you intend to hurt?"

Farrow's breath caught in her throat. "I . . . I . . . don't know what you . . . mean," she stammered.

"I think you do," Yama stated. He released her arm and gazed at the area illuminated by the lantern. "How will they work it?"

"I don't know what you're talking about!" Farrow cried.

Yama looked at her. "Keep your voice down!" he warned.

Farrow was chilled by the iciness of his tone. She sensed her world was coming apart at the seams, and she was panic-stricken.

"Did you take me for a complete imbecile?" Yama demanded in a hard whisper.

"I never—" she started to say.

"I will admit," he said in a brittle, incriminating manner, "I was stupid enough to fall for your charade. I actually believed you cared for me! How dumb can I get!"

But I do! Farrow wanted to scream, but she couldn't bring herself to speak the words. She was overwhelmed by the stunning realization she'd been wrong all along. He did really and truly like her!'

"—but I couldn't understand why you were so tormented," Yama was telling her. "I tried to reason it out. I concocted a hundred and one excuses to justify your behavior." He made a contemptuous sound. "I allowed myself to think you were troubled because of your affection for me! You didn't want to commit yourself, knowing you would be returning to your own people! You already had someone special and didn't want me to know!"

"I don't have anyone—" Farrow mumbled, but he ignored her.

"And then today!" Yama said. "I see you at breakfast, and you won't even look at me, let alone converse! Why? I asked myself again and again. There was no rhyme or reason to the way you acted. I began to wonder if Plato and Rikki were right. They've been suspicious of you from the start, although Rikki gave you the benefit of the doubt. Before he left, Blade told us to keep an eye on you. Not to trust you." He paused, his voice lowering sadly. "Not to trust you! And I went and developed deep affection for you!"

"But—" she began.

"And now you show up here! This late at night!" Yama cut her off. "Why? I wondered. You were shocked to find me on duty. You wanted Ares to be here. Why? Because you knew I would suspect something was up. Ares doesn't know you as well as I do. He might accept your line about wanting fresh air. But I don't!"

Farrow fought back an impulse to burst into tears. "Yama . . ."

"Shhhhh!" he cautioned her.

"Yama . . ."

Yama glanced at her, his face creased by lines of misery. "Don't talk!"

"They'll be using infrared goggles," Farrow informed him. "They can see in the dark."

Yama studied her for a second, then took her hand and pulled her down to the third step. He crouched and tugged on her hand. "Get down!"

Farrow squatted beside him. Their heads were now below the rampart and invisible to anyone scaling the west wall. "I'm sorry," she said in his right ear. "I—"

He placed his right hand over her mouth. "Not now. Later."

Farrow stifled a sob. She felt utterly helpless, a prisoner of her own emotions, unable to intervene, bound by her duty as a Technic soldier on one hand, and her love for Yama on the other. She couldn't violate her Technic oath, and she wouldn't betray Yama. There was nothing she could do but ride it out and hope for the best.

Yama looked at her. "Thanks for letting me know about the goggles," he whispered.

Farrow nodded, biting her lower lip. The demolition team would use a grappling hook and come over the northwest corner, where she was scheduled to meet

them. What would Sergeant Darden do when they
climbed the wall and discovered she wasn't there?
Abandon the mission? Not very likely. Darden was
dedicated. He would complete his assignment with or
without her.

Yama had his left ear pressed to the top step,
listening.

Farrow suddenly perceived the reason for the lantern.
Yama was brilliant! Anyone coming over the wall would
have a dilemma to resolve: what to do about the light?
They could shoot out the lantern, but the Warriors
would be alerted. They could circumvent the lighted
portion of the rampart, but to do so would entail
avoiding the stairs. And the stairs were the only means
of reaching the inner bank, unless they dropped a line
into the moat and swam across, a difficult proposition
when carrying a backpack and field gear. No, the wisest
recourse would be to leave the lantern alone, and
attempt to reach the stairs undetected.

Only Yama was waiting for them at the top of the
stairs.

Farrow tensed as a faint scuffing reached her ears.
Was it Darden and the demolition team? She closed her
eyes and performed an act she'd never done before; she
prayed Darden would realize the lantern was a ruse and
decide to abort the assignment.

Yama angled the Wilkinson barrel upward.

Her eyes now adjusted to the gloom, Farrow could
distinguish Yama's features. She wanted to reach out
and tenderly caress his cheek, to let him know she was
sorry for her stupidity. The turmoil in his tone had con-
vinced her of his sincerity. There must be a perfectly
reasonable explanation for the incident with the petite
brunette. She would ask him about it when this was
over.

There was a muffled thump from the northwest
corner of the rampart.

Sergeant Darden and the demolition team had
arrived!

Farrow could scarcely breathe, dreading the impending conflict, waiting for Yama to make his move. She

clenched her hands until her nails bit into her palms.

Yama raised his ear from the first step.

Farrow knew whatever was going to happen was going to happen soon. And she realized there was a chance Darden was aware someone was on the stairs. His ear amplifier might have detected Yama's breathing, or hers for that matter. If Darden had, his squad would have their Dakons trained on the steps. They would shoot at anything that moved. Yama would be cut to ribbons.

Something nearby clicked.

Farrow suddenly reached out and grabbed Yama's right arm. He glanced at her in surprise. "I love you," she whispered, then, before he could move to stop her, she unexpectedly rose, facing the rampart. Facing Darden and the three members of his demolition team.

Sergeant Darden was nearest the lantern, perhaps four feet to its right. Private Johnson, the loudmouth, was two feet from Darden. The one whose name she couldn't remember came next, not six feet from the steps. And Rundle, the plastics expert on the squad, was only two feet away, her Dakon II leveled, her finger on the trigger. She saw a shadowy form abruptly rise in front of her, and she instantly fired, the Dakon set on automatic.

Farrow was staggered by the impact. She felt an intense burning sensation in her chest, and she was flung across the stairs and against the opposite railing. Her left arm caught on the top rail, at the elbow, and she dangled limply with blood pouring from her wounds, her eyes riveted to the rampart, as Yama rose, his voice roaring a strangled "*No!*" as the Wilkinson chattered, and Private Rundle was smashed backward by the force of the slugs tearing into her body. Yama swiveled, and the unidentified trooper took several rounds in the face and was catapulted to the rampart. Sergeant Darden and Private Johnson opened up, but their target was already in motion, darting up the stairs and rolling across the rampart, coming erect near the lip, and the Wilkinson burped, slamming Private Johnson from his feet and hurling him over the edge and into the swirling moat below. Farrow saw Darden frantically pulling his Dakon's trigger, and she recognized the gun was jammed. He dropped the Dakon and went for his automatic pistol. Farrow was amazed by what transpired next. She gaped as Yama tossed his own gun aside and rushed toward Darden, darwing his scimitar in a streaking, fluid blur. She could see the terrified expression on Darden's face as he drew his automatic and tried to aim at the Warrior. But Yama was quicker, and he slashed the scimitar down, severing Darden's gunhand from his arm. Darden opened his mouth to scream, and Yama flashed the scimitar crosswise, splitting Darden's throat wide open, crimson gushing over the commando's neck, and then Yama sliced the scimitar into Darden's abdomen, once, twice, three times and tolled, and Darden's intestines spilled over his pants and legs as he futilely clutched at his stomach. He slowly sank to the rampart, gurgling and spitting blood.

Yama glared at the fallen Technic for a second, then whirled and raced to the stairs.

Farrow tried to grin as he dashed up to her. "Nice," she mumbled feebly. "Real . . . nice."

Yama dropped the scimitar and took her in his arms. "Don't talk!" he cautioned her. "Help is on the way! The Healers . . ."

"No," Farrow said weakly. "Too late . . ."

"Don't say that!" Yama said, his voice raspy.

"Need to know . . ." Farrow stated in a ragged whisper.

"What?" Yama asked, his face an inch from her.

"The girl . . . this morning . . ." Farrow managed to squeak.

"The girl? What girl?" Yama declared, perplexed, in anguish. "You mean Marian? My niece?"

"Niece?"

"My brother's daughter," Yama said. "What about her?"

Farrow eyes widened. "Your brother's daughter . . ."

"I don't see . . ." Yama began, then paused as an

intuitive insight flooded his mind. "You didn't think she and I . . . ?"

Farrow mustered a smile. "Never . . . was too bright." She coughed, blood smearing her lips and chin. "Kiss me. Please."

Yama bent down and touched her lips with his own. He could taste the salty tang of her blood on his lips and tongue, and then she stiffened and gasped, expelling her dying breath into his mouth.

Yama felt his eyes moisten, and he buried his face against her left shoulder.

It was another minute before footsteps pounded on the stairs, and Rikki-Tikki-Tavi appeared, gleaming katana in his right hand. He reached the third step and paused, then proceeded to the rampart. Shouts and yells were mingling in the compound below. He scanned the bodies, then moved down to Yama's side. "Yama?"

"Go away." The voice was muffled by the fabric of Farrow's shirt.

"Are you all right?"

Yama's response, when he finally answered, was tinged by an immeasurable melancholy. "No. I'll never be all right again."

The day was marked by a bright sun and a clear blue sky. The drawbridge was down as a party of Hunters prepared to leave the Home. Although the Family included four Hunters in its ranks, the Warriors frequently assisted in hunting the venison so necessary for their continued survival. The four Hunters were hard pressed to find the quantity of game the Family required, and they gladly welcomed any help the Warriors offered.

Rikki-Tikki-Tavi was on duty on the west wall, watching the Hunters preparing to depart. The Hunters and one other. Yama had volunteered to go along. Rikki suspected Yama needed the activity, needed to do anything to take his mind off Lieutenant Alicia Farrow. They had buried her four days ago with full honors.

A muted whine arose from the west.

Rikki looked up, elated to see the SEAL traveling toward the Home at breakneck speed. "Alpha Triad is coming!" he called out. "The SEAL is coming!"

The word spread like wildfire. Family members were running toward the drawbridge. Rikki could see Plato in the vanguard. And there was Sherry, Hickok's wife, carrying little Ringo. And Jenny and Cynthia, Blade's and Geronimo's spouses, toting their children. And all of the other Warriors except Teucer, who was on the north wall, and Ares, who had agreed to fill in for Yama on the east wall.

The SEAL rolled from the trees and across the field,

up to the lowered drawbridge. It braked and the engine was shut off.

Blade vaulted from the transport, a beaming smile on his face. He surveyed the assembled crowd and spotted his wife. "Jenny!" He ran forward and clasped his wife and son in his arms.

Geronimo was next to emerge. He jogged the ten feet separating the transport from the gathered welcomers, and took his wife in a tender embrace.

Rikki saw Sherry staring apprehensively at the SEAL. He glanced at it, suddenly worried, wondering why Hickok hadn't appeared. He cupped his hands around his mouth. "Hey! Where's Hickok?"

Geronimo released the raven-haired Cynthia and crossed to the transport. He leaned in the passenger-side door. "Wake up! We're being attacked by mutants!" he yelled, and stepped back.

A sleepy Hickok stumbled from the SEAL, his Pythons in his hands, swinging the revolvers from left to right, seeking the mutants. It took a moment for the reality of the situation to dawn on his fatigued senses. When the Family began laughing at his stupefied reaction, his face turned a livid scarlet and he glared at Geronimo, holstering the Colts. "I should of known! You never can trust an Injun!"

Geronimo, chuckling, draped his right arm around Hickok's shoulders. "I wish you could have seen your face!"

"I know what I'd like to do to yours!" Hickok groused.

Sherry and Ringo hurried toward the gunman.

"I want you to know," Geronimo said as she neared them, "we had our chance and we blew it."

Sherry, too relieved at finding her husband returned and unharmed, paid scant attention to Geronimo. "Oh?" she replied absently.

"Yeah," Geronimo said as Hickok hugged his family. "We could have left him back on Highway 94, but Blade insisted we had to pick him up. Personally, I think the walk back might have done him some good.

Get rid of that flab . . .'' He stopped, realizing his barbs were being wasted.

Hickok and Sherry were kissing passionately.

Rikki grinned, delighted at the arrival of his three companions. Now Blade could assume command of the Warriors, and things would go back to normal, the way they should be. His eyes happened to alight on Yama.

Not everything would be the way it was.

Rikki thought of Alicia Farrow, and of his own beloved Lexine, and he thanked the Spirit she was safe, ever eager to share her love and laughter with him. He saw the Family milling about Alpha Triad, happy, engaged in lively banter.

All except one. Yama was walking toward the forest, Wilkinson in hand, going hunting.

Rikki sighed. He knew, given time, Yama would recover. Time, so the cliche went, healed all wounds. Which was true. But Time couldn't erase human memory, couldn't deliver a person from periodically experiencing pangs of heartfelt grief. What was it that religious book in the library had taught? ''The supreme affliction is never to have been afflicted. You only learn wisdom by knowing affliction.'' Which must make Yama, temporarily at least, the wisest man in the universe.

Enough!

Rikki dismissed such somber reflections from his mind, and watched a cardinal winging on the wind. Affliction might be inevitable, but life went on. Life invariably went on.

And such was the way it would always be.